SCORE

St. Martin Family Saga

Gina

Watson

ISBN-13: 978-1941059005

CONTENTS

ACKNOWLEDGMENTS

Several people made this endeavor possible. Without their support this fictional world would not exist. Thank you for all the motivation and support. Beth Hill at *A Novel Edit* is wonderfully professional and does a marvelous job with the editing process. Emily Colter and Maxamaris Hoppe at Waxcreative truly did an awesome job at conceptual design for the website that channels the St. Martin Family. Damonza.com handled cover design and formatting. Mom and Karen, thank you for always agreeing to proofread. Monica your continued support and motivation were priceless on this project. Beth B. thank you for always giving it to me straight, this is invaluable to an author. To all my students and friends, this would not have happened without your beta skills: Kayla H., Courtney W., Danielle S., Meagan W., Ruth L., Angelica L., Jenna L., Tammy S., Kelli R., Amber S. Brian, what can I say, you put up with me, for that there are no words. Thank you.

CHAPTER 1

Chloe Mills groaned at the piercing light invading her sleep and at the ungodly troll driving spikes into her brain. Then she gasped at the low raspy moan funneled into her ear from the body next to her. *Shit!* Damn Las Vegas and their pleasure slogan. What happened in Sin City might stay there, but the repercussions could easily trail the sinner for a lifetime.

Chloe's gaze darted around the room, taking in its tattered and faded gold wallpaper, stained beige carpet, dirty walls, and squealing air conditioner.

Lifting the covers to peek underneath, she winced to find herself naked, that nakedness canceling out any hope she had that maybe, just maybe, she and the guy in her bed had been too drunk to have sex.

God, she didn't even know who he was. She hoped her friends hadn't let her go off with a scuzzy stranger dripping some disease.

To her right lay a beautiful naked male body with long lean muscles and bronzed skin. As she scanned his sinewy chest—a six-pack plus—she congratulated herself that at least she'd chosen an Adonis to pleasure herself with. Too bad she couldn't remember anything about the pleasuring. Her eyes followed his lean torso down to his manhood, currently fully engorged.

"God," she whispered and dropped the bedding. He was impressive.

He moaned again and she looked to her right, but his forearm shielded his eyes, and she couldn't make out his face. Unfortunately, she could recognize one highly distinctive feature—the tattoos on his triceps. Only it couldn't be. God help her, it better not be. For the love of all that was good and holy—and for the sake of his balls—the man sharing her bed better not be Caleb St. Martin.

She looked again, only to have her worst fear confirmed. It was, in fact, Cal. *Oh my God*, she thought as she pushed at his body underneath the

1

covers. Her efforts were futile—the man was a solid wall of stone. She snatched her hand back when contact with his warm body caused an electric current to buzz through hers.

She'd spent a good part of her adolescence and young adult life pining after Cal. She'd purposefully wander onto his family's land and wait for him in the climbing tree or at the tree house designated *St. Martin boys only*. He'd tolerated her in their early years but as they got older, he'd taken to being a bully. She'd spent hours dreaming and doodling *Mrs. St. Martin* in her journal. Then reality hit. She'd heard through her friends of his conquests at college. Thank God the university was large enough she never had to witness his exploits once she started going there.

"Get up!" she cried.

He swore low and raspy. Voice dripping with an eroticism that had her quivering, he said, "What's your problem, woman, didn't you get enough last night?" He grasped her hand under the sheet and held it to his erection, rubbing up and down. "I'm good for another round if you're up for it."

He sizzled in her hand, and she pulled back as if she'd been burned. "Oh! You, you, bastard. I can't believe you brought me to this seedy motel and took advantage of me."

His eyes were closed as he lay languidly, a smirk on his face. "You were the one sticking your tongue in my ear at the casino last night. Couldn't keep your hands off me."

"I hate you, Caleb St. Martin." Chloe swung her legs from beneath the covers and stood as her anger began to build. She continued her rant all the way to the bathroom as she stomped off in search of her clothes.

***

Watching her storm into the bathroom, Cal could definitely appreciate the curves Chloe had picked up since her tomboy days. Her ass was lush and full, just the way he liked them. He recalled the warmth of those luscious globes in his hands last night. *Damn!* He went painfully hard just thinking of her body.

Cal stretched, remembering how much fun he'd always had picking on Chloe. It was quite humorous the two of them had ended up in bed together. They'd always hated one another. Growing up on the neighboring property in Whiskey Cove, their little hometown outside of Baton Rouge, Cal had always delighted in playing practical jokes on Chloe. He didn't understand why he enjoyed teasing her so much, but it certainly gave him great pleasure. Perhaps it was the way she always took herself so seriously that made it fun. Right now she was banging things around in the bathroom and talking to herself. He always knew she was a little odd. Was she giving herself a pep talk?

As Cal pushed himself up on his elbows and then slowly sat up, he squinted at the light pouring in from the gap in the dusty and threadbare curtain. What Chloe had said was right—this was a seedy motel and a shitty one at that. At least he could have taken her to the Bellagio. He scratched his head, trying to recall how the events of last night played out. The memories were foggy. He stood and stretched, then looked down into the wastebasket and idly counted the condoms there. Six? Not possible. Had they done it six times? *Fuuuuuck!*

Cal strode to the bathroom and pushed the door open, startling Chloe and confirming that yes, she was in fact giving herself a pep talk in the mirror.

"And you will put this night behind you and get your degree."

With a lazy smile, he walked to the toilet and lifted the seat. He pulled himself into position. "How are you feeling?"

"What the hell are you doing?" she screeched. "Don't look at me! Where are my damn clothes?"

The shrillness of Chloe's voice sent needles into his eye sockets. He braced himself with his free hand on the wall above the toilet. "Will you stop yelling. I gotta take a piss, and it's a little late for modesty, isn't it?"

She went into a full-on diatribe. "How am I feeling? I had sex with Caleb St. Martin, the devil himself. I don't know if we even used protection. God, I don't want to catch your diseases."

Cal turned his head in her direction. "I don't have diseases and we used protection. Six times."

Chloe gasped.

"How do you feel physically?"

Chloe's body bowed and tensed. Cal mentally braced for the onslaught of her wrath.

"You can save the fake compassion. It's not like you ever cared about my welfare before."

What? He'd known Chloe her entire life—of course he'd looked out for her. But she was always a bit peculiar. For instance, why was she so mad about last night?

"I don't know why you're acting like this. You should be thanking me. Since you were with me last night, you're safe. If you had woken up next to someone else, who knows what would have become of you."

After relieving himself, Cal turned toward Chloe and watched her glorious and full raspberry-tipped breasts sway with the rage that coursed through her. His eyes narrowed, and he felt himself go hard.

Chloe had started pacing the floor in front of the vanity. She turned toward him with a distinctly angry snarl on her face and her fists clenched at her sides.

"You're so fucking arrogant. I can't believe I ever even thought I

wanted this. Plus, I don't even get to remember what happened last night."
Her frantic pacing picked up speed. "And since college you've been fucking
every girl that smiled at you. You're a man-whore. And God, what if I get
pregnant? Cal! Are you even listening to me?" She looked down his body.
When she took in his arousal, her arms crossed her chest and her lips
tightened.

Yeah, she was ticked, but she was also aroused. Her nipples hardened
and lengthened before his eyes. Cal swallowed the lump in his throat. "Not
listening. Too busy watching your tits grow hard."

He ducked when Chloe threw a Nevada-shaped glass ashtray at his head.
It hit the wall behind him and crashed to pieces on the floor.

Chloe was gone when Cal got out of the shower. Stubborn woman.
He'd told her he had called a cab, told her they could ride to the airport
together, but she'd left anyway. Finding her clothes had taken a few
minutes, and she'd grown hotter with each second. The door had been shut
on her shirt, and her thong panties had hung from the fan. Cal had tried to
keep those as a Vegas souvenir, but Chloe had gone ballistic and he thought
he'd heard her sniffle, so he'd given them back and apologized. He'd pulled
her bra from behind the television and handed it to her without a word.

Now he made sure they hadn't left anything, and then he too headed for
the airport. He met up with his buddies at the gate.

Cory, his brother, and Alyssa were there, along with his friends Dean
and Bradley. They'd come to support another of Cal's brothers in a poker
tournament. Cash was doing well for himself, and Cal and Cory had wanted
him to know they were behind him. They'd also wanted to party, but only
after Cash had gotten the message of family support.

He focused on Alyssa, wondering if she knew about last night. He
assumed she would since she and Chloe were friends. Her greeting of a
raised eyebrow confirmed his suspicions.

"Alyssa." He nodded at her and then at Cory. "Where is she?"

Alyssa tilted her head. "She doesn't want to speak to you."

His gaze followed Alyssa as she stomped to the newsstand nearest their
gate. Magazines in her hand, Chloe stood waiting to check out.

Cory turned to Cal with wide eyes. "Dude, you scored with Chloe.
That's fucking awesome. I bet that was a hot piece of ass."

Cal roared. "Watch your fucking mouth."

Cory raised his hands in submission. "Sorry, just thought you'd be
happy to have won the bet."

Shit! It hit Cal like a heavy fist to the jaw—last night his buddies, Cory
included, had bet him he couldn't get Chloe in the sack. He recalled Cory's
exact words: "Dude, Chloe hates you. You have a better chance of sneaking
into the White House and getting it on with the first lady."

"Please tell me Alyssa doesn't know about the bet."

4

Cory looked down at the floor.

"Damn, Cory!"

Cory slowly lifted his head and met Cal's eyes. "Sorry, dude, but yeah, I kinda let it slip last night."

"You had sex with Alyssa?"

Cory shrugged. "I was drunk. This morning I told her under no circumstances can she ever tell Chloe."

Cal shook his head slowly as he turned to the newsstand. "This is not going to end well."

Bradley and Dean joined them. "Hey, guess what? Bradley just got shot down by this flight attendant who was de-planing. She told him if he didn't stop harassing her, she'd put him on the no-fly list."

"Dude, that's outrageous," Cory said with a wide smile. "So guess who got it on with Chloe last night?"

Cal popped Cory in the back of the head.

Rubbing at his head, Cory said, "What the fuck?"

"I told you to keep your damn mouth shut."

Dean said, "Uh, we already know."

Going lightheaded, Cal asked, "How the fuck do you guys know?"

Bradley looked to both Cory and Dean, then frowned at Cal. "You texted us."

Cal pulled his phone out of his pocket and glared at it. He quickly deleted the messages.

Cory shrugged. "What's the big fucking deal? You won five hundred bucks."

"No!"

"What?" Dean asked.

"No money, no bet. We don't speak of this ever again. Is everyone clear on that?"

The men murmured their agreement. Cal pulled his brother close and said, "And you keep Alyssa's mouth shut."

"How the hell am I supposed to do that?"

"By not being the dick you usually are."

Cory crossed his arms, looking just as obstinate as he had been when they were young. Cory screwed a lot of women without ever looking back. It could create problems, especially in a town as small as Whiskey Cove.

"You'll have to play nice. Take her out a few times, let her down easy so she doesn't retaliate."

Cory's eyes narrowed. "No can do, bro. That woman's overly dramatic in the sack. You know how I hate that."

"Cory, please. Can you make just one sacrifice to help me out?"

"Shit!" Cory stomped off.

Cory'd take care of Alyssa as well as he could. Which meant that Cal only had to deal with Chloe.

He leaned against the wall, his eyes fixed on her as she approached. She refused to look at him, even angled her body away from his when she sat.

She was still mad. Fine. She deserved to be. He recalled her angry speech from earlier. Yeah, mad was a mild word for what she'd felt. But she'd revealed more than anger. She'd admitted that she thought of him. Just as he'd thought of her. Her words hadn't been all that coherent when she'd been ranting, but her admission indicated she'd thought about them being intimate. Course, then she'd gone and called him a man-whore. That was harsh. He wasn't really, promiscuous. He'd just done what every other male did at college—gotten drunk at parties and headed off with a girl.

Just because it had been a different girl at every party didn't mean he was a man-whore.

He crossed his arms. She could pretend he didn't exist for now, but that shit wasn't going to fly when they got home. Chloe Mills wasn't going to ignore him for long. Not after sharing her bed and her body with him.

He shifted when he grew hard at the remembered perfection of her body. He needed to get to the bottom of her wanting.

No, she wasn't going to write him off. Six condoms said there was something between them, something worth exploring.

And the next time he explored Chloe's body, he planned to be sober. He intended to not only imprint himself on her so she wouldn't so easily be able to turn away, he intended to brand his memory and his own body with her every response and her scent and her flavor.

CHAPTER 2

Chloe had graduated with a degree in marketing. The only problem was, she couldn't obtain a job in this market. That was how she found herself back at Louisiana State University majoring in speech pathology. She was in her last semester and currently finishing her internship at Baton Rouge General Hospital.

She'd been working with her patient Steve LeBlanc and his wife and two daughters. The stress was taking a toll on her, though she'd never admit it. Her family and the LeBlanc family attended the same church. While watching her patients struggle was difficult, that difficulty was magnified a thousand when she knew her patient. Chloe had cried herself to sleep more than once because of Steve's bleak prognosis.

Steve had been diagnosed with Lou Gehrig's disease more than two years ago. Chloe had been working with him for so long now that it was hard to remember Steve had been a healthy thirty-six-year-old with a solid real estate career and a growing family. To look at him now one would never believe there had been so much life behind those blue eyes. From his hospital bed, he observed his girls and his wife when they came to visit. And that was all he could do—watch. He couldn't even eat as those muscles had been taken from him too. He received nourishment through a tube, and the subsequent weight loss left him unrecognizable to even his closest friends.

Chloe witnessed a hint of a sparkle in his eyes whenever he looked at his wife, which always comforted her. She hoped Sharon could see it too. Sharon LeBlanc had been strong these last few months, watching as Steve's condition had deteriorated to the point that now the only muscles he could control were those that innervated the eyes. He'd gone down fast, so fast it was hard for Chloe to keep up. She had to continuously adjust his communication device. At first he was able to supplement his speech with use of an alphabet board. When he could no longer use the speech muscles, Chloe had ordered a speech output computer, but Steve couldn't even use that device anymore. God knew she tried to be encouraging, but she understood the moment he'd told her he had no fight left in him and asked her to look after his girls, all three of them. She'd told him it would be an honor and he needn't worry. He said he knew they would be in good hands.

Today Chloe was seated at Steve's bedside in the hospital where she interned. The girls, Sarah and Riley, and Sharon were there. They were talking about getting frozen yogurt on the way home. Sharon worked nights now that Steve no longer had income, and Chloe watched the girls on the nights Sharon worked. Tonight she'd have the girls. Chloe had offered to help monetarily so Sharon wouldn't have to work, but Sharon wouldn't hear of it. The entire town knew Chloe's family had money, knew it wouldn't be missed, but Sharon had refused. She'd taken on Steve's role as provider for her family, trying to make their lives as normal as she could. Chloe couldn't fault her for that.

***

You spent four thousand dollars on video equipment boy?

As Cal walked into the hospital where Chloe worked, he deleted his father's text. He wondered what it would be like to have a father who believed in his work. Cal was finishing his coursework for a graduate degree in film studies, loving what he did, jazzed about the possibilities that technology brought to the art. His professors told Cal he was talented, said he had the drive and the skills, even the insight, necessary to make a name in the field, but Clifton St. Martin wouldn't know anything about that, not having attended his son's academic awards banquet. Not having been interested in most of Cal's projects.

Cal shrugged it off. His dad had his own interests and dreams, and they'd never matched Cal's. He'd been hoping for his dad's acceptance since he'd been a teen, but he'd been disappointed every time. He didn't know why he expected anything different from the man.

He shook off the familiar and pointless thoughts and turned his mind toward Chloe. That subject brought pleasure rather than disgust.

Cal had thought of nothing but her over the last few days since his return to Baton Rouge. The image of her that night in Vegas haunted his dreams, and he wasn't concentrating very well in his classes either. He was supposed to have turned in his master's thesis outline but with his every thought consumed by Chloe, he was behind. Every morning he woke hard as steel. He could recall her every sound during the height of his possession of her body. He remembered how her sweat-streaked skin glistened in the moonlight filtering in from the window in the cheap motel. He remembered the feel of her muscles as she contracted around him. He remembered her heat. And he'd been hard ever since. He'd even resorted to whacking off in the shower, something he hadn't done since his teens.

He'd called, texted, and emailed Chloe since that night, yet she refused to respond. He was glad to have an excuse to find her—her expensive Tag Heuer watch had made it into his belongings. Given the extent of what was some serious marathon sex, Cal guessed how that could have happened.

As he neared the nurses station, Cal saw a face he hadn't seen since the last time he was at church, Easter morning. "Mrs. LeBlanc. It's nice to see you."

When she saw him, she smiled warmly. "Caleb, please stop making me feel old and call me Sharon."

Caleb leaned over to give her a hug.

The nurse behind the counter ogled Cal, her eyes slowly studying him. He was used to the reaction and smiled. He didn't add any heat to the smile, however. He was looking for Chloe, not a woman interested in a thrill or a quickie in some empty closet.

The nurse greeted Cal with a large toothy smile and bright eyes. "What can I do for you today?"

Cal checked out the nurse's nametag. "Nancy, I'm looking for Chloe Mills. Am I in the right place?"

Sharon tugged at his sleeve. "In fact, you are. Come with me."

When Sharon and Cal stopped at the door to Steve's hospital room, they saw Chloe hoist a big camera to her shoulder.

"Okay, girls, climb up on the bed next to Daddy." The girls squealed and did as they were told, looking up at Chloe with wide grins. "And where is it you want to go when we leave here?"

In unison they answered, "Ice cream!"

Chloe's muffled voice answered from behind the large camera. "Ice cream? I thought you said you were in the mood for broccoli and brussels sprouts." More squeals came from the girls.

Cal stood alongside Sharon, taking in the scene. He remembered his father telling him something about Steve LeBlanc being ill, but he'd had no idea it was this dire. Cal remembered Steve had worked with the St. Martin family quite a few times over the years. He didn't look good now. In fact, he was hardly recognizable as the man Cal had known.

Cal wondered about the old VHS camcorder Chloe used and asked Sharon about it.

"Chloe lent me a digital recorder, but it got stolen out of my car so she brought in this old one. She's making videos for us so the girls will remember their father when they're older. It's really a godsend because I wouldn't have even thought of it with everything else that's going on." They both turned back to the girls in the bed.

Chloe slowly lowered the heavy camera. When she saw Cal, she blushed furiously. Voice breathy, she said, "What are you doing here?"

He reached into his pocket. "I'm returning your watch. I tried calling and texting, but you won't answer me."

With his statement, and the fact that he had her watch, he'd just revealed they'd been intimately involved, but he couldn't help himself. He'd always loved to goad her.

She didn't disappoint—a blush bloomed and worked its way across her cheeks and down her neck. She laid the camera on a chair and strode to Cal to retrieve her watch. With clenched fists and tight lips she said, "Thank you."

Cal shifted. Damn, just watching her walk, hearing her voice, aroused him.

From the bed one of the girls asked, "Why do you have Chloe's watch?"

Cal knelt beside the bed and answered, "Because Chloe's a silly-willy girl who forgot to put her watch on this morning and she needs it for work." The girls laughed at him. Steve made eye contact, and Cal nodded. The girl closest to Cal reached her hands out and leaped into his arms. Steve's eyes filled with liquid. Cal didn't know what to do. He simply stood staring at Steve with a wiggling girl in his arms. Seconds ticked by.

Chloe cleared her throat. "All right, girls, it's time for us to get going. Tell your mom and dad goodnight and meet me in the hallway." Chloe hugged Sharon and said goodbye to Steve. Cal followed her out to the nurses station.

Just being near her brought back erotic memories from that one night. Cal moved even closer. Closed his eyes and inhaled her scent.

Chloe tapped into a computer nestled into a nook against the wall, and Cal stepped back to give her privacy to update Steve's chart. But he watched her every gesture and nuance, hoping for a sign that she was as affected by his presence as he was by hers.

Chloe's head turned to meet his gaze. Her brow rose. "Cal?"

"I like ice cream."

"You want to go with us?"

"I do."

"Why?"

"Don't be difficult. Can I come?" Softer, Cal added, "Please, Chloe." He knew he was pleading. Hell, he was almost begging. He needed to be with her again. He'd either get her out of his system or he would make his condition worse. His hope was to ensure they didn't let years of hate smother their burning desire.

Seeing her care for the LeBlancs humbled him. Chloe was a woman and no longer the overall-clad girl of his youth. She was selfless and giving, a woman of both strength and compassion. She nodded and when the girls came out, he joined their adventure.

They treated the girls to pizza and then took them for the coveted frozen yogurt. Once they reached Chloe's condo, they bathed the girls, Chloe washing while he dried. Then he and Chloe took turns reading the Berenstain Bears, but the girls were asleep before they could finish the book. Watching Chloe care so tenderly for the girls had Cal's mind engaged in way too many unwanted images and thoughts. The one that confused him the most was the mental picture of her with her own children. With *their* children. Did he want to have children? The thought of Chloe's belly big and round with his child made him think he might. He knew one thing for certain—he would enjoy the conception.

Chloe's condo was tastefully decorated in Danish contemporary. The kitchen, living area, and office were all open and flowed fluidly into one another. The color scheme was black and white with pops of royal and aqua blue. It was comfortable and warm, like the woman who lived there.

When they finally settled in the living room with glasses of wine. Cal said, "Sharon tells me you're making videos for the girls."

"She was worried they wouldn't remember their dad, so I started making the videos a while ago. I've downloaded them to my laptop." She sipped her wine. "It's a good thing too, because someone stole the digital camera from her car."

"How do you plan to edit the film?"

"I hadn't thought to do that. It might be nice though. I have a ton of footage from the earlier years of his life—some video, some stills."

"Do you want me to take a look at it? I don't mind editing it for you."

She tipped her head and offered a tired smile.

"Actually that would be great if you could."

They sat on opposite ends of the couch, sipping wine. Listening to the silence. Cal watched Chloe intently. Occasionally she'd make eye contact with him.

"Have you thought about that night?" he asked, when his desire to know overcame his fear of her reaction.

When she shifted, he prepared for her response. But he was looking forward to it. Chloe's responses were always worth watching.

She fondled the stem of her wine glass as she fixed her eyes on him. Her tongue darted out of her mouth and moistened her bottom lip. "My memory has been busy filling in the gaps resulting from the alcohol-induced amnesia."

She rotated her shoulders back and straightened her spine, accentuating her breasts as she did. She definitely remembered something. Otherwise her body posture wouldn't have been so open. So affected, so sensual.

Holy fuck, she wanted him. She was practically preening. But it wasn't like he wasn't affected by her too. He sat up a little straighter, put his glass

11

on the table. He'd been growing hard as he watched the memories of that night play across her features.

He wanted to touch her long silver-white curls, but he wouldn't stop there. He knew he wouldn't. She had full breasts and hips and he could remember her soft curviness. Her body could tempt the most God-fearing man, so he didn't stand a chance. He remembered going down on her, and he wanted another taste. Now. He wanted her flavor, her essence, on his tongue. He wanted to be inside her. Wanted to touch and taste and fuck her until they both moaned with pleasure.

Her hazel eyes grew smoky when she climaxed. He remembered that as well. Those daring looks from the corners of her eyes got him hot again and again, one reason, obviously, for the six condoms—a new record for him. He wanted to experience all of that again, experience her. She was so small and he so tall that she rode him in all the right places.

While he'd been reminiscing, she'd apparently been doing a little mental imagining as well. Her cheeks were flushed and her eyes had grown dark. *Damn.* Game on.

He moved next to her on the couch, reached for her wine glass and put it next to his on the table. He bent his head as if meaning to kiss her, but stopped short. With his mouth hovering over hers, he said, "I want you."

Chloe gasped and her chest rose and fell rapidly. She whispered, "I want you too, but I need you to be clear on something."

Her voice was determined, and Cal was disoriented as he was yanked from the cusp of passion and thrown into stark reality. "What?"

"I don't want you making fun of me like when we were kids. I'm not a girl anymore. I enjoy sex, but I won't ever let you touch me if you bully me like that again."

Cal was dumbfounded. He stared at her, mouth wide. Had she been harboring resentment all this time? He didn't remember what he'd done, yet she was clearly still upset about it. He couldn't imagine hurting her now. Had he then? He swallowed the lump that formed in his throat. "Chloe, I'm sorry. I never intended to upset you. I was a child. You're definitely not a girl anymore. I intend to treat you as the beautiful and seductive woman you are."

His hand cradled her neck, and he nipped at her mouth until she opened on a breath, allowing him to tease her with his tongue. The kiss started out sensual at first, but then the intensity grew until they were both gasping for breath. His hand slid up the silky cream-colored blouse she wore. The sheer material clearly displayed her hardened nipples and needy state. He pinched the distended tips, and she moaned around his name. He pulled her blouse over her head and reached to adjust his aching penis. She had him hard and hot. He unclasped her bra and slid the fabric sensually down her arms, exposing her beautiful milky globes. Perfection. He grasped both breasts and rubbed his cheeks against her hardened nipples and then started using his lips. He took one nipple between his teeth and rolled it gingerly.

Touching her, tasting her, was better than he remembered. Better than he'd dreamed.

He was distracted when Chloe pulled at his shirt. He helped her by lifting his arms, allowing her to pull it over his head. Cal watched her eyes track across his chest. When she was done, she lowered her head but peeked up at him with big eyes and a sly smile. She was fucking perfect. Cal shifted them until they lay on their sides, facing one another. Sharing the same breath.

"Chloe, feel what you do to me." Grasping her hand, he moved it to cup his aching erection. She cried out, "Oh my God," and he shushed her, reminding her not to wake the girls.

He unbuttoned her shorts and slid his hand between her thighs. "God, you're dripping." He started massaging her clit with his thumb. When her eyes turned smoky, he pushed his middle finger into her cunt. Moaning, she closed her eyes, but Cal didn't want that. He wanted her to see him when she came. "Chloe, keep your eyes on me; don't close them."

She opened eyes smoked out with a dark hazel rim. Knowing what that meant, knowing that she wanted him, made him even harder. Her mouth opened slightly and released a deep moan, and Cal let his index finger join the first, stroking into her heat. He increased the pressure on her clit, and her body began to writhe. She started softly chanting his name, her voice deep and hoarse. Her cunt squeezed his fingers like a vise, and in response he curled his fingers up to massage her G-spot. "Come on my fingers." She cried out once at his words and then again when she came. He smiled with satisfaction, but leaned toward her, trapping her face against his chest, and whispered "Shh." He massaged her gently until the last waves left her body. Then he slid his fingers free and licked each clean. She tasted like fucking honey.

Chloe's eyes were heavily lidded. "Cal, take me," she demanded.

She didn't have to tell him twice. He was on a mission to satisfy this woman. He put some space between them, wondering if he was crazy. It had never been like this with a woman. But he didn't stop. He couldn't. He slid her shorts down, along with her panties, and revealed her beautiful bare sex. She was made for him. Made for riding his cock. She helped him remove his pants and boxers and then took him in her warm hands and started working him.

"I want to taste you."

God, he wanted that too.

He maneuvered so that she was atop him and opened his arms wide in invitation. She slid her curvy little body down between his legs, stroking him all the while. Then she lifted her head and grinned. His cock jumped and his hips lifted. God, she was going to kill him. The anticipation was going to kill him.

"Chloe," he groaned.

She looked back down at him and slid one hand under his shaft to fondle his sac. Then she did what he'd been waiting for. She licked the head of his cock, swirling her tongue around and tasting him with long strokes. When she finally sucked the tip into her mouth, he moaned, loving the way her lips slid sensuously over his glans. Her hot mouth cradled his cock halfway down before she pulled back, sucking all the way.

Cal growled her name, latching on to her hair, and she sucked and massaged with more aggression. She took more of him in her mouth, but still not all of him.

"Can you take it all Chloe? All of me." He rolled his hips, wanting to thrust but not wanting to hurt her.

She smiled—he felt her lips move—and then she took him deep. His fingers tightened in her hair, helping her. Guiding her. Tugging and pushing to show her the rhythm he needed. Just when he thought he was going to die from pleasure, she took him all the way to the back of her throat, her tongue tracing the underside of his cock from back to tip.

"Jesus, Chloe!" He shuddered, tightening his muscles. He didn't want to come yet. Not yet. "I love fucking your mouth."

She pulled back and then increased her pace yet again, alternating fisting and sucking him. When he was close, he called her name on a groan, and she closed her mouth around just his tip. He came with a furiousness he never had before as she used her fist to pump his shaft and milk him. He tried to come quietly, but she was like a fucking warm moist glove, and he cried out her name at the same time come shot from his body.

They lay spent, with Chloe cradled between his legs. After a few minutes, she said, "I need you inside me." She maneuvered herself atop him and rubbed her wet pussy lips up and down his cock, moistening it. She tried to settle on him, press his cock inside her heat, but in their narrow space on the couch, she couldn't drive her body past the crown. Cal was enchanted as he watched her lithe movements, as she adjusted her hips to take him. Then he was undone when she looked at him with heavily dilated pupils and whispered, "Help me."

Cal grasped her hips and tugged her down while thrusting up with his own hips. She cried out, and her body tensed. Fearing he'd pushed too hard, Cal said, "Did I hurt you?"

"No, just give me a minute."

After a few seconds, she started to rock, slowly and smoothly. Sensing her need, he moved his hips beneath her. She rocked in a steady, sensuous rhythm. Her large breasts swayed above him, causing his mouth to water. He needed to suck on the beautiful globes.

"Lean down to me." He lifted himself to meet her halfway. He sucked her beautiful raspberry-tipped nipples—one, then the other, then the first again—while she rode his cock.

The hard nipples and her milky soft skin, her hypnotic rocking, drove him to the brink of insanity. He needed release now. He flipped their bodies so she was beneath him. Chloe sighed and watched him from under heavily lidded eyes. That was all it took. He pistoned into her at a frenzied pace, pulling her knees up so that his sac slapped against the lips of her pussy. Heaven. He was balls deep inside little Chloe Mills from next door. God, he couldn't believe that all this time heaven was just beyond the lake. What a fool he'd been. His scrotum drew up, and he tensed.

"Are you close?" Damn, please be close.

She rocked hard and fast against him. "God, yes."

"Together, okay? Look into my eyes."

Three more hard thrusts had him emptying his hot fluid into her. Chloe writhed beneath him, and her contractions drew every last drop from his cock. Cal collapsed on Chloe and kissed her brow. And then he tried to settle his whirling world.

Head lowered and resting next to hers on the couch, he was afraid he'd gotten carried away. Her eyes were closed and her chest rose and fell quickly. "Christ, I'm sorry. Did I hurt you?"

Chloe grasped his chin and directed his gaze up to her face. "Never apologize for something so beautiful. Of course you didn't hurt me."

He kissed her mouth lightly. "I thought I got carried away is all."

She kissed him back. "You did, but I like being carried away."

He started to laugh and she asked, "What is it?"

"I was just thinking if we had spent more time doing this and less time arguing, things may have been different."

"Different how?"

"I don't know." He stared into her eyes, wondering what she thought behind them. "Maybe we'd be together." His finger traced designs on her bare stomach.

"You mean we would be together like a couple?"

"Yeah, like a couple. We wasted a lot of time, don't you think?" Cal sat up and pulled Chloe around until her knees straddled him.

Eyes locked onto his, she asked, "Are you saying you want to be a couple?"

"I think we owe it to sex, don't you?" He offered her a devilish grin and nipped at her breast.

"The sex is"—he could tell she was searching for a particular word with her head cocked and her distant stare—"otherworldly."

His grin turned into a full smile. "*Otherworldly.*" He locked his hand to her hips, as if to shift her from his lap. "That's going on Twitter right now.

I've not been described in quite that way before."

She slapped at his biceps and reclaimed her spot on his lap, pressing even closer. "So are we gonna date now or what?"

"Yes, Miss Mills, that's how I operate. I'll date you, fuck you, assist you with any other needs you may have. You can do the same for me. From time to time I may buy you something pretty."

She smirked. "I just like to know where I stand going in, that's all."

He whispered, "Where you stand is next to me."

Big hazel eyes filled with liquid as she smiled softly. "Next to you."

"Next . . . to . . . me . . . " he whispered between kisses.

Then he took her bottom lip between his teeth and lightly sucked. His tongue nudged her lips apart, and he kissed her long and deep. She gave as good as she got, plundering his mouth with her tongue. They stayed entangled for several minutes. He grew hard, and then they dove in for round two.

CHAPTER 3

Despite her subconscious telling her to not be, Chloe remained hopeful whenever she thought of Cal. He'd had to sneak out in the early morning because it wouldn't have done to have the girls asking questions. She and Cal had been entangled all night, even during slumber. He was due to come over tonight to look at her footage of the LeBlanc family and outline a plan for the home movies. For the first time, Chloe felt like she was doing something truly useful for the LeBlanc family. She dared to hope that maybe the films might be finished before Steve passed on. The doctors said he could go any day now. The respiratory muscles had shut down a while ago, and he'd been on a ventilator. Eventually he would succumb to pneumonia.

At the hospital, Chloe was ending her day and charting treatment progress. She pulled her cellphone from her pocket to log the time. It showed five unread texts. She touched her finger to the message icon and the messages were revealed. *Miss yr sexiness already.* That had come in at 7:28. *Can still taste U*—8:30. *R U ignoring me?*—9:22. *I guess U R*—9:34. *U don't like being bothered at work? See U 2nite, wish U a wonderful day, counting minutes til we meet again!* That last one had come at 9:45. With a smile stretching her face wide, she replied, *Not ignoring U, just busy, I feel the same way!*

Was Cal serious when he spoke of a relationship? God, she'd always wanted that, dreamed of that. Her face heated when she recalled one of the most embarrassing moments her attraction to Cal had caused. It was his eighteenth birthday—he was older than her by five months—and she'd gotten him a gift. Cal had always loved taking pictures and making videos, so she'd purchased a novelty item, a camera that took and developed pictures and spit them out in the form of stickers. She'd dressed for the occasion. Shaved, primped, curled, tweezed, and polished for him, wanting him to recognize how grown up she'd become. She'd worn a sleeveless

17

black cocktail dress and patent leather pumps. When she'd found him, on top of a ladder, changing a light bulb on the front porch of his home, he did a double take. For a moment he took her in and no words were spoken. She thought she saw an increased heat and intensity in his eyes, but then he'd said, "What the hell are you wearing?" She'd felt so small. She'd wanted the ground to open up and swallow her down. Still she'd given him his gift and they'd messed with it for a while before he tossed it aside, complaining that it took the most horrid pictures.

The whole evening had been ruined for her.

And yet apparently he'd changed.

Chloe put her phone in her pocket and thought how different Cal was from other guys she dated. Men usually kept their feelings hidden. So he was quite atypical. Yet . . . She looked at her phone. Had his text said he missed her? No, he said he missed her sexiness. He was counting the minutes to more sex. Well, truthfully, so was she. She'd be a fool if she weren't. And so what that she was a little mixed up? She couldn't wait to see him, whatever the reason.

She finished up and rushed home to shower and change.

At 6:30 sharp, Chloe's doorbell rang. She opened it to reveal Cal leaning in her doorway, his smirk dripping with sex. He wore black dress slacks and a white oxford shirt, sleeves rolled to his elbows. He sported an industrial-looking watch on his wrist, and his light brown hair was styled into a messy bed-head look. With lowered eyes, his long dark lashes cast shadows across his cheeks. His sexy, playful grin could melt panties, and Chloe felt hers moisten with need.

"Chloe" he said as he handed her a bouquet of pink tulips.

She smiled. And then she blushed. "My favorite." But he would know that.

"I remember Mom constantly complaining that a certain little blond-haired girl kept sneaking into our yard and stealing her tulips."

The heat in Chloe's face went up a few degrees. Cal reached his hand out, brushing her cheek.

"You're blushing. Cute."

She cleared her throat. "Please come in."

"What smells so good?"

"I've got tilapia blackening in the oven. I made rice and gravy too. And"—she pressed both hands to her hips—"my grandmother brought over some yeast rolls."

"Shut up, woman!"

Chloe smiled, put the tulips down, and lifted the foil on a pan of rolls so Cal could take one. He took two instead, immediately biting into one. "Hey, don't fill up on rolls."

"Mmm, I'm going to ask for your grandmother's hand in marriage."

Chloe laughed as she watched him enjoy the rolls. When given the chance, he'd always stolen hers when they were kids. She'd remembered that and called her grandmother this morning to see if she would prepare a batch.

"And now you don't have to thieve them away from me."

"Thieve what away?"

"The rolls. You always snatched my roll from my lunch."

"I never did that!"

"You *always* did that."

Cal smiled and demolished the second roll in two bites.

"It was only because I secretly wanted to have otherworldly sex with you."

Chloe threw the kitchen towel at his head.

She opened the oven door and bent over to peer inside. "I think just five minutes mo—" She jumped. "Oh!" Cal had come up behind her, had reached one hand between her legs and wrapped the other arm across her chest. When she angled her face toward him, his tongue swept into her mouth, causing her to go breathless. He growled when she pulled away, but she said, "The gravy will burn."

"Let it burn." His voice was low and raspy.

"Just give me a second." She pulled the pan from the heat and turned in his arms so he could kiss her properly. He kissed her as if he needed her breath in his lungs. She'd never been kissed so deeply before. His tongue plundered every available surface, licking and tasting. All she could do was cling to his shoulders as he held her and thrust in and out of her mouth.

Chloe's chin and cheeks were hot and raw from the five o'clock shadow of whiskers on his face, her lips full and plump when Cal finally pulled back.

"You look gorgeous. I can't keep my hands off you. When you're not in my arms, I feel like part of me is missing."

His revelation rendered her speechless. They stared into one another's eyes. This new Cal disoriented Chloe, and she was afraid he was getting deeper into her system than was safe. When he was with her like this, she could see herself so easily loving him—if she didn't already. She closed her eyes and inhaled a deep cleansing breath. "Do you want to eat?"

He kissed her nose and released her. "I'd love to. I wasn't expecting a fancy meal. When you said we'd get together, I figured we'd order takeout."

Chloe looked him up and down. "I like your dress clothes."

Cal smiled. "Yeah? I'll keep that in mind. I was out with Cory doing some groveling for his business."

Furrowing her brow, Chloe said, "Groveling?"

"You know he just set up his veterinary practice in Whiskey Cove, right? We were doing some marketing. Actually, I don't know that we accomplished much of anything outside of getting Cory additional numbers for his black book. The town's gone crazy. Every local mama wants to set Cory up with her daughter."

Chloe laced her hands behind Cal's neck. "Envious much?"

He smiled his panty-melting smile, revealing pearly white and straight teeth. She loved his smile. "How can I be envious when I've got you in my arms?"

He nuzzled and nipped at the shell of her ear. "Mmm, you smell like vanilla, and the scent drives me crazy." He inhaled. "I just wish Cory would take it easy. He's burning through women at an alarming rate. I guess he isn't solely to blame, but I don't want him to get into trouble."

"Cory will make his own way, and I'm sure he'll make a few mistakes as he does. We all do. But I know one sure thing about St. Martin men."

He rubbed her earlobe between his thumb and index finger. "Oh yeah, what is it you know about St. Martin men?"

"They own their mistakes."

When Cal was ten, he'd accidentally driven a golf ball through one of the windows of her house. He'd been escorted by his father to fess up and to offer to help with chores around their house, as a form of punishment, she guessed. She'd heard Clifton St. Martin say to Cal, on her front porch, "St. Martin men own their mistakes, son."

Cal grimaced. "You sound like my father." His eyes fixed on something in the distance.

"Cal?"

He smiled and kissed her chastely on the lips. Then he earned a squeal and a swat from her when he patted her on the behind.

"Get the food, I'm hungry."

He set the table with the stack of dishes she'd laid out on the counter, and she put her tulips in water, adding them to the setup. She served him two pieces of fish and dished out the rice and gravy. Cal uncorked a bottle of chardonnay from a local winery and filled their glasses. Watching them eat together, anybody would have thought they'd been together for years.

Chloe considered Cory's new vet practice. "I don't mind helping Cory with his marketing needs. You know I have a degree in marketing."

"That's right." Cal's brow hitched.

"What?"

"I don't think I want you anywhere near Cory."

She shrugged. "Suit yourself. So how's your dad been?"

It was Cal's turn to shrug, "Pretty good, I guess."

"You don't see him very often, do you?" She knew he didn't.

"There's really no point. He doesn't approve of or maintain any interest in what I do."

"You mean video and film production."

Cal narrowed his eyes. "That's exactly what I mean."

Should she press? When he blew out a long breath, she decided it might help. "Do you maintain an interest in his business?"

"What's that supposed to mean?"

She called on all she could recall from Geology 101. "Well, if both sides of a shelf are pushing, it creates a bow, you know, like with tectonic plates. Wouldn't it be better if one side gave in a little and let the other pass?"

Cal stared intently at her, almost glaring. "Are you saying I should quit the art program and go work for my father?"

"No, never! Is that what you heard me say?" She drank some wine. "I'm saying you might consider sharing an interest in his business to prevent damaging your relationship beyond repair."

"Why should I do that when he couldn't give a shit about my work?"

"I have no answers for you, Cal, other than to suggest it might be better to get along with your father than to risk being at odds with him all the time. What if something were to happen and you never cleared the air?" She shrugged, hating to see him fighting with his dad.

Cal dropped his fork, his eyes wide. "What's going to happen to him?"

"Nothing. I meant hypothetically." Chloe shook her head. "Never mind."

They cleared the table. Chloe washed the dishes and to her surprise, Cal dried and put them away. He refilled their glasses and they moved to the office area of Chloe's living room. She drew a heavy box from under the desk.

"I pulled all the video I had."

Cal pushed her aside to lift the box.

"I marked and dated all the tapes. They're in chronological order."

"Wow, there's a lot of footage here." He rummaged through the box. "Is it all from before he got so sick?"

"Actually, there's a good mixture."

Cal turned to her "Hey, I was thinking of doing a documentary of sorts, with some interspersed family footage. I was hoping to use the film to spread the word and educate people about ALS—what it is, how it progresses, and current research. What do you think?"

Eyes tearing up, she smiled at him. "I think that would be a wonderful use for the footage."

He exhaled long and slow. "Good, I'm glad you like the idea." He bit his lip, looking uncertain, and then stepped closer to where she was seated in her white desk chair. "I'd like to use the project as my master's thesis. Do you think that would be okay?"

Chloe shrugged. "I don't see why it would be a problem, but I'll ask Sharon, if you like."

"That would be awesome." He nuzzled her neck. "Hey, what are you doing tomorrow?"

"I'm taking the girls to the zoo."

"Oh." He nodded. "The zoo." His shoulders slumped and his lips turned down.

"Yes." Chloe was laughing inside, fighting to not let it show. He was pouting like a small child who'd been left out of a family outing.

His head went lower by the second. Chloe rubbed his arm. "Cal, you're welcome to come with us."

A huge panty-melting smile erupted across his face. "That would be great. What time?"

Giggling, she answered, "Eight, to beat the heat." She stood and moved to the couch. Cal watched her.

"Sounds good. I'll be here." He raised a suggestive brow. "Or maybe I'll just still be here?"

"That was smooth, Mr. St. Martin."

"Smooth enough to work?"

"Hmm . . . I think so."

"Great news, Miss Mills." He smiled again. "Great news." He turned and walked to the kitchen. He opened the pantry door, then the refrigerator.

From her position on the couch, Chloe asked, "What are you looking for?"

"Something sweet."

"Oh, I forgot about your sweet tooth? I don't have much of anything like that. I hadn't planned on dessert."

"This'll work." Cal returned to the couch with a vanilla pudding cup and a spoon. He slowly pulled back the foil top on the pudding cup. "Take off your clothes."

Chloe's mouth fell open, and her breathing became shallow. Cal sat on the couch next to her.

"Chloe, come stand in front of me and take your clothes off." He smacked his lips as he licked the pudding from the foil. "I want my dessert."

With shaky fingers Chloe set her wine on the end table and stood where Cal was indicating, between his long legs. He dipped the spoon into the pudding cup and then lifted it toward his mouth. Halfway up to his mouth, he flipped the spoon upside down. He sensually inserted it into his mouth and slowly pulled it out on a savory moan. "Strip for me."

"You're distracting me."

Cal looked up at her, his eyes twinkling. "Sorry, my bad."

With trembling hands, Chloe began unbuttoning her linen shirt. The breathless anticipation was almost too much to bear. She took a deep breath as she parted the shirt's sides and slid it down her arms. She started on her jeans, but Cal shook his head.

"Nuh-uh, bra next. I want to watch your breasts sway and your tits grow long and tight as you work on the other things."

God, when he talked to her like that, warmth pooled in her belly and she could feel herself grow wet for him. She unclasped her bra, slid it down her arms, and let it fall to her feet. She felt the heaviness in her breasts, telling her they were swollen. She took a deep breath—a shaky breath—and her chest rose and fell with the motion. His eyes grew instantly darker.

"You're aroused; your nipples give you away. You have the most beautiful, enticing nipples." He rubbed his lips together. "You're so aroused you're shaking. Finish."

Chloe undid her jeans and shimmied them down her legs. She needed to undo the straps on her platform sandals to remove her jeans. She knew Cal was turned on by her ass. She further knew she wore a thong and that the Mills women had rather full, round butts. She turned 180 degrees and bent at the waist to unhook her shoes. Cal growled and mumbled expletives under his breath, the deep satisfaction of turning him on causing a grin to break across her face. Once she removed her sandals, she slid her pants the rest of the way down her legs and stepped out of them, kicking them out of the way. She bent at the waist again and hooked her thumbs beneath the waistband of her thong underwear and pulled them down in a painfully slow drag.

The moment Chloe sensed something cold and wet on the lips of her pussy, she gasped.

"That's right, you can't tease me like that and not expect a reaction," Cal said. "Stay still, just like that. You're going to be my dessert, baby."

She braced her hands on the coffee table as he continued to paint her with pudding. Putting his hands on her hips, he pulled her back to his mouth, causing her to bend forward more. Chloe could feel cold air on her sex. He dove in and there was no delicate manner about it. Cal's face was wedged between her thighs as he lapped up the pudding with his tongue and pushed his fingers inside her.

Then he stopped. She moved to straighten up, thinking he was done, but the pressure he exerted with his hand on her back told her to stay put.

"Don't move."

He applied more pudding to her aroused sex and this time he slathered all of her, including the puckered bud of her ass. He started licking from there and trailed down her seam, culminating at her clit. His tongue tip flicked the hardened bud.

He pressed his fingers inside her, not easing the ache, but instead making her gasp.

"Oh God," she wailed.

He found her G-spot with ease.

"Chloe, massage your clit."

He wouldn't have to tell her more than once this time. She rubbed herself with frenzied strokes, needing release instantly. He whispered low in her ear, "Slow down, we have all night."

"Cal, I need you."

His warm breath bathed her ear. "I'm right here, baby."

She felt more of the cool pudding at the tightly coiled ring of her ass. When his finger breached that muscle, the pressure slammed her entire body into orgasm. On a whispered moan, she chanted his name. He nibbled her earlobe and breathed heavily into her ear. "Yeah, you like that don't you, baby. You're coming, fucking my fingers so good." He increased the speed of his strokes inside her pussy and curled his fingers, and then she came on his hand. When the waves subsided, Cal removed his fingers and got into position behind her. He slid his cock through her wetness and entered her, seating himself fully on the first plunge. Chloe cried out at the sudden fullness and intensity.

A low growl escaped Cal's lips. "God, your snug little cunt is like a vise around my cock. Do you feel that?" He pulled out excruciatingly slowly.

"Yes, I feel it." God, did she feel it. "Uh, Cal?"

"Yeah, baby." He was panting, sounding nearly breathless.

"I want you to fuck me hard."

"Be careful what you wish for." Grasping her upper arms, he pulled her up with his large masculine hands and plowed deep. Using the leverage he had on her, he forced his way into her body at a pace that had her seeing stars. The image of her breasts jolting in the decorative mirror on the wall across the living room had her entranced. His sac made a slapping sound on every thrust as he slammed into her with violent velocity.

Chloe didn't want to be treated like a delicate wilting flower. She sensed Cal holding back, but she wanted him to take her with authority. Given her situation with the LeBlancs at the hospital, she wanted and needed to feel life. She wanted passion in all things. Cal had always been passionate. When he really wanted something, like his videos, he'd stop at nothing until he consumed it or it consumed him.

When she started to spasm around his cock, he finally lost control. He turned her to the couch and they kneeled on it so she could use the back of it to steady herself. His hands slid up her torso to grasp her breasts. He thrust his hips hard, so hard that the couch bumped against the wall. He pulled her tightly against him, until the length of their bodies were fused, and his warm seed burst into her.

She lost herself for a few minutes and only came back when, still connected, Cal pulled her with him to sit back on the couch.

"Fuck." His breath was just easing. "Damn, Chloe."

They sat recovering a few moments more. Chloe didn't know when she'd ever been as well ridden. She doubted that she'd ever felt so good after sex.

He had removed his shirt and they were skin on skin as she sat in his lap, her back to his front. She felt him when he shifted to look around her.

"Hand me my pants. I have something for you."

Intrigued, Chloe leaned forward and snatched up his pants. He pulled out a box in the telltale Tiffany blue that any woman would recognize. He held it up to her in his palm. When she took it, he clasped his hands together just under her breasts.

Chloe pulled the white ribbon and opened the box. Inside was a silver keychain with a silver heart attached. Chloe lifted it from the box. The heart was a working timepiece. The bezel was trimmed in diamonds and rubies. "It's beautiful."

"I thought if you were to forget your watch for work, you would still have your keys. And now you'll always have the time."

"It's a very thoughtful gift, Cal. Thank you." Cal treating her in such a gentle manner overwhelmed Chloe, and a few tears escaped her eyes.

Cal grasped her chin and turned her face to his. "Hey, what's this about? You're supposed to be happy when I give you jewelry." He smiled sweetly and wiped her tears away.

"I've wanted this since I was a child. I had finally given up on us when I started college. So many emotions are zinging through me right now, it's no wonder that I'm a bit tearful."

"Hey." Cal lifted Chloe to face him, finally severing their intimate connection. "I should have tried harder. I understand now—pushing someone away is not the same as letting someone go. I thought if I could push you away then I wouldn't want you any longer. That never happened. I wanted you still. I've always wanted you. Instead of suppressing the want, I pushed you away and hurt you. I was young and a fool. Say you'll forgive me."

Chloe lowered her lips to his and kissed him with a slow and light touch. Her eyes met his. "I forgive you, Cal."

They fell asleep in her bed and sometime during the night they woke and made slow, gentle love. After that they talked and dozed off, loosely spooning. Chloe woke to Cal rubbing his thick cock through her folds from behind her. To her mind, it was the best morning she could recall. He pushed his hardness into her. In that position he felt enormous, and Chloe shivered at the fullness. God, he felt so good, as if he belonged inside her. As if his body was claiming hers. As if hers claimed him.

His hand slid up her thigh and pushed her top leg higher on the bed. She trembled. He whispered, "Take me," into her ear and then penetrated her with steady strokes until she whimpered his name. His hand slid around her and over her abdomen, landing on the tight bud where all sensation coiled. He began to massage her, and Chloe came with him for the fifth time since last night. They couldn't get enough of each other.

Without pause, Cal rolled her over and plunged into her for one last round before they had to get ready for the zoo. This time was different. This time they were eye to eye, and his pace was sensual and steady, not frenzied or hurried, but just right. Sunlight stole through the curtains and Chloe watched it light the planes of his face, glinting in his morning stubble. He kissed her tenderly and cradled her neck with care. When they came he whispered, "I never thought it could be like this." Chloe couldn't answer because she'd been overcome with unfamiliar emotions.

They showered together and dressed for the zoo. Chloe was distracted, guessing she might be venturing into dangerous heartbreak territory, just like when she was younger and they were neighbors. She just hoped Cal didn't spook this time. Her heart would never recover. But this time if he bolted, she wouldn't go down without a fight.

CHAPTER 4

Cal and Chloe were standing in front of the polar bear exhibit with Riley and Sarah. They'd been there for twenty minutes. Chloe leaned over so just Cal could hear.

"Riley can watch the polar bears for hours, and Sarah has just discovered a picture of penguins on that sign." Cal looked in the direction Chloe indicated. Sarah took off running and squealing, hell bent on finding the penguins. She stumbled and fell and started to cry. Cal ran to her and pulled her to her feet.

"Up you go." He knelt in front of her and inspected the scrape on the back of her arm. "Hmm, looks like regulation grade road rash. You should be okay." He turned her arm to expose healthy skin and bent to place a kiss on it. "All better?" Sarah nodded and he stood. Her cherubic face looked up at him.

"Will you be my daddy?" she asked.

He looked over to Chloe. At Sarah's question, the inner corners of her brows rose and her lips parted slightly. Chloe made several attempts to speak, but no words came from her twitching lips. She shook her head. He guessed the little girl was trying to come to terms with her father's illness. He knelt in front of her and removed his sunglasses.

"Sarah, I would be honored to be your daddy, but your father needs you right now. He needs you to be strong and happy. I'll be here and so will Chloe, but you need to hug and kiss Steve as much as you can, okay?"

"Okay, but he doesn't hug or kiss me like you do."

Tears immediately fell from Chloe's big doe eyes. She knelt with them. "Sarah, your father wants to hold you very badly, but he can't because he's sick. Honey, look at me." She pushed Sarah's hair out of her eyes. "He can still hear you and he sees everything you do. He loves you, sweetheart. And he's so very proud of you."

Riley, the younger of the two girls, asked, "Miss Chloe, why are you crying?"

"It's okay, Riley, I'm just talking with Sarah." Looking back to Sarah she added, "I want you to tell me you'll hug and kiss your father bunches." Chloe wiped at her eyes.

"Will that make you happy?"

"Yes, very happy."

Cal rubbed Chloe's back in support.

"Miss Chloe?"

"Yes, Sarah."

"Is my Daddy going to heaven soon?"

Chloe's body shuddered and the tears ran steadily from her eyes. "Yes, sweetie. Soon he won't be here like he is now. You understand that, don't you? That's why you must love him while he's here. Your daddy needs your love. You must squeeze and hug and kiss him bunches and bunches."

Cal felt her compassion and love radiate out to the girls.

"Okay, I'll hug and kiss him bunches." She giggled. "I'll tickle him too."

Chloe smiled. "That's great. And you too, Riley. You hug and kiss your daddy bunches too."

Riley nodded again and again, her ponytail bopping up and down like the tail of an excited dog.

Cal handed Chloe a handkerchief. She ran her finger over the embroidered initials. "Caleb Dean St. Martin," she whispered. She tipped her face up at him with one brow raised. "You carry hankies?"

He shrugged, "I have allergies."

She started to laugh, deep bone-cleansing laughter. He chimed in and so did the girls.

Chloe had always been a humanitarian, fighting for the weak. At school she would place herself in harm's way to diffuse a fight or argument, even if it meant she had to suffer the attack. As he watched her with the girls, he thought about the fragility of life. And he thought about what she'd said about his father, about how he should give a little. He could do that, couldn't he? What would it hurt to appear interested in the family business? It could hurt some, but hell, it hurt being at odds with his father. He decided her idea was worth considering.

After the zoo they dropped the girls at their house and went by his apartment to pick up clothes and toiletries. Now that he'd found Chloe, he couldn't bear not to be around her. At her apartment they settled in for the night, with Cal at Chloe's desk utilizing their computers to review the film.

He worked for two hours and stood to stretch. He walked to Chloe at the dining table and put his arms around her. She'd been working on constructing a large communication board. On the board were clear pictures of the LeBlanc family and of him and Chloe and even the

LeBlanc's cat, Sir Thomas. She'd made three columns: pronouns, verbs, and adjectives. A lot of the words on the board conveyed an emotion.

Cal pointed. "What's this?"

"It's a new board for Steve. He doesn't use the computer anymore; I think it has become too laborious. But with this he can use an eye gaze to express mood and desire to his friends and family. I'm going to introduce it tomorrow. I thought it might help Sarah if she could see him communicate by using his eyes." Chloe shrugged. "It may not work, but I thought it worth a shot."

Cal pointed to the board again. "So does Steve understand all of this?"

Chloe nodded. "That's the worst part about Lou Gehrig's disease—the mind remains unaffected."

He had no idea it was that way. He knew Steve tracked movements with his eyes but he just lay in the bed. So his brain was unaffected, yet he was trapped inside a useless vessel. Cal was immediately humbled. He didn't know how Chloe was able to remain motivating and positive as she watched his decline from day to day. She was a light wherever she went, shining especially bright where it was darkest. She always had been.

Using his camera phone, he took a picture of Chloe as she explained the board. Then he stroked her hair. "It's amazing what you do for them. You're wonderful."

He bent and kissed the top of her already shaking head.

"I feel like I've done so little. Some days I feel utterly hopeless. I can only imagine what the girls and Sharon must feel."

"I think the last time I saw Steve was two years ago. He had worked with dad on some real estate endeavors. He looked so normal. I had no idea his body had become so . . . so debilitated. I thought whatever he'd been diagnosed with was going to progress slowly, or I imagined he was going for a treatment—a cure. When I saw him, I was devastated. We can get so busy living our lives and not thinking about our health. It just kind of put things into perspective for me." He sat across from Chloe. "I don't know what I would do if that happened to me. I don't know how Sharon is dealing with it all. I wouldn't be able to cope if my spouse were deteriorating in front of me and there was nothing I could do."

Chloe studied her board and nodded. "I've thought the same thing. I think Sharon knows she has to be strong for the girls, but I know she cries at night when she's alone and I have the girls. I can see it in her face the next day."

Cal reached across the table to clasp Chloe's hands. "This weekend I'm going to visit my father."

Chloe smiled. "In Whiskey Cove?"

"Yeah. I'd love it if you'd come too."

"I'll be there. How long has it been?"

He let his breath out slowly and leaned back in his chair. "Too long . . . I guess about two years since I've been home. Anyway, this weekend dad's throwing some kind of mixer for casino bigwigs. They've completed another mega-structure."

"Is that the attitude you plan on having while you're there? Sort of a Debbie Downer, isn't it?"

She grinned and stuck out her tongue. Cal leaped from the dining room table just after she did it, but he was still too slow to catch her. He finally managed to corner her in the living room. He tackled her to the floor and tickled her senseless.

"Ahhhhh. Cal stop. I'm gonna pee, I swear it."

He stopped, but pinned her beneath him. He moved her silver-blond curls from her face and gazed into her eyes. He left a peck on her nose, each eyebrow, and each eyelid as he made his way slowly to her lips. He took her bottom lip between his teeth and sucked. She removed his shirt before removing her own shirt and bra. Then, wordlessly, he sucked at her nipples until they grew hard and needy. They removed each other's shorts and underwear. He leaned against the couch and she straddled him, slowly pulling him into her warmth. Once he was fully sheathed inside her, she started to undulate up and down on his cock. With his hands on her hips, steadying her, they made slow, sweet love, banishing his vague fears about illnesses and meeting with his father.

***

The closer they got to the St. Martin Ranch in Whiskey Cove, the more tense Cal became. Chloe cleared her throat. "So . . . does Mr. St. Martin know you're coming to this mixer?"

"He does not."

Chloe raised her brow. "Why didn't you tell him?"

Cal thought he knew why. He didn't want to think it was the only reason, but he didn't think he'd have been able to take any rejection or condescension his father may have hit him with, so he'd opted to not share his plans. "I just didn't get around to telling him."

Chloe nodded and pressed her lips together. "Will any of the other boys be here?"

Jesus, why was she asking him all these questions? It made him nervous; his palms had started to sweat. "I don't know."

She grasped his hand. "Cal, talk to me."

Couldn't she see he didn't want to talk about it? Didn't even want to think about the reception from his dad.

He sighed. "Some of them will be there. Cory will be. Of course Camp will be at the forefront of all the festivities since he works for my father. I think Logan is serving his special *Good Doctor Brew* in honor of the occasion."

"I'd heard Logan opened a craft brewery. I've yet to try the beer. Is it good?"

"Oh yeah, it's real good. He's got his bestseller that he makes with special hops he gets from Germany. It won the US Open Beer Championship. And before you ask, yes, that's a real award and it's a big fucking deal."

"Is that the one called *Kidney*?"

"No, it's the *Spleen* brew."

"A doctor turned beer brewer—that's funny. I heard there's a *Penis* and a *Vagina* brew too."

"That's actually true."

They laughed together.

When they pulled into the long driveway, Cal parked under an old pecan tree, cut the engine, and looked toward Chloe. "I want to thank you for coming with me. I don't think I would have done it otherwise."

Chloe put her palm to his cheek. "I'm glad you're home."

Cal pulled their bags from the back and motioned for Chloe to move toward the house.

At the front entry, Cal opened the heavy double doors and they walked through. He tossed their bags at the bottom of the winding staircase and they crossed the marble foyer to the kitchen. When they rounded the corner into the kitchen, Cal froze. Alyssa sat on one of the stools. Chloe greeted her and appropriately asked what Cal couldn't get out.

"What are you doing here?"

"I could ask you the same thing."

"I'm here with Cal."

Alyssa eyed Cal coolly. No, *coldly*. Fuck! Cal knew he should have told Chloe about the bet. He'd started to a number of times, but things were going so well he wasn't ready for the fight he knew they would ultimately have and that would be within her right to begin.

Alyssa shrugged. "And I'm here with Logan."

"Logan!" Cal said a little louder than he intended. "What happened to Cory?"

"I wouldn't know. I told you, I'm here with Logan."

This was so not good. "So is Cory here then?"

"I may have seen him out on the lawn." She waved at the wall of windows at her back.

He peeked out onto the lawn and did in fact see his father dictating directives to Cory and Logan. He desperately wanted to speak with Cory, but there was no way he was leaving Chloe alone with Alyssa. Alyssa seemed quite unhappy about something. He would guess things had not gone well with Cory and that she was in full retaliation mode and now poor Logan had been dragged into Cory's no-strings-attached sex life. Cory was older than Cal by eleven months, but he could have been the youngest if they went by sheer maturity.

Feeling anxiety twisting his muscles, Cal turned to Chloe. "I guess we should go out back and say hello to my father."

Chloe smiled. "Sounds good." She jumped down from the stool she'd been sitting on and told Alyssa she'd see her around.

Alyssa replied, "Don't do anything I wouldn't do."

What an absurd line, given the circumstances. Chloe was nothing like Alyssa—to Cal's utter relief.

They made their way out onto the lawn where the bandstand had been setup for the festivities. Cal looked at the handsome man with eyes so similar to his own. His father was tall and sported a thick head of nut-brown hair that had started to gray at the temples. He had big dimples and a large, toothy smile. Cal knew he would look the same in thirty years. As soon as his father saw him, he greeted him with a smile.

"Son, it's been entirely too long since you've been home. What do you say we put our differences aside?"

His father reached an arm out and Cal went toward it. His father hugged him with ferocity, squeezing the breath from Cal. Cal choked up.

"So great to see you, son. And who is this you've brought with you? Is that little Klepto Chloe?"

"Dad!"

"Oh, come on. Chloe knows I'm joking."

Chloe went into the waiting arms of Clifton St. Martin, and he squeezed her tight. "Don't you, girl."

Chloe smiled. "Yes, sir, but just for the record, I've told Mrs. St. Martin multiple times how sorry I am about stealing her tulips." She clasped her hands and lightly lowered her head. "It's no excuse, but they were exquisite."

Cal's dad threw his head back and laughed. "Chloe est tres belle."

Looking at Chloe, Cal responded, "Oui pere, elle est tres belle."

Chloe smiled and blushed. Cal was aware that Chloe knew enough French from living in these parts to know they were discussing her beauty.

His father regaled Cal with updates regarding his commercial contracting business and Cal realized he was genuinely excited for his father's success.

Cory joined them and their dad put his arm around each of his youngest sons.

"Did you hear, our Corrigan's got the entire town in an uproar? The women, that is."

Cal hitched a brow at Cory. "I may have heard something about it. Did you know one of his most recent disastrous conquests is now sharpening her claws on Logan?"

More laughter erupted from Cal's dad. "Oh, to be young and feel love's sting."

"I'm not so sure this has anything to do with love."

Cory folded his arms across his chest and looked down his nose at Cal. "You don't need to act so high and mighty. Sometimes what you do isn't an act of love either. Wasn't there some sort of bet you had going?"

Cal snarled at Cory and reared back to punch him, but Cory ducked.

"Fuck off, Cal," Cory said.

"Cory, I need to speak to you in private." Cal grabbed his brother by his upper arm.

Cory sighed heavily. "Whatever."

Cal looked to Chloe. "Will you be all right out here for a few minutes?"

"Sure. I'm just gonna walk over to my house and say hey to my folks."

A great idea. She'd be out of the way for a while. "You can take dad's LSU golf cart," Cal offered.

Cal retrieved the keys from his father, but he withheld them from Chloe until she returned his kiss.

As she drove off in the direction of her childhood home, Cal whirled to Cory. He looked around and then lifted his chin, indicating a spot away from other ears. When they were alone, Cal said, "What the fuck is going on? Why is Alyssa here looking as if she could spit nails?"

"Well, brother mine, it turns out Alyssa is bat-shit crazy. I'm talking *Fatal Attraction* crazy."

"And yet you let her get her hooks into Logan."

Cory looked to where Logan was currently setting up beer kegs at the bar area. "Poor bastard never saw it coming. I'm just as shocked as you to see her here. I'd no idea she'd been getting boned by Logan."

Cal started rubbing his brow with his thumb and forefinger. "Shit, it's only a matter of time before she tells Chloe about the bet in Vegas."

"Dude, if I can make a suggestion . . . " Cory rubbed his index finger across his upper lip and then snapped his fingers. " . . . Tell Chloe before Alyssa can get to her."

Cal shook his head. "Gee, thanks, Cory, that's profound." He left Cory sniggering at him and wandered around, studying the setup his dad had commissioned for the party. He greeted Logan, but there was nothing for him to do. And he was only delaying the inevitable.

Cal took off to walk across the property. He stopped to play with a couple of puppies that ran after him, not wanting to rush Chloe's time with her family, but he eventually ended up on Mills land. He planned to speak with Chloe regarding the night they hooked up in Vegas. It was time he came clean about the bet. He just hoped their relationship had come far enough that it could see them through this snag.

The obscenely decorated golf cart caught his eye as Chloe was heading back on the path toward St. Martin land. He waved to her and she turned in his direction.

"Hey, stranger." She greeted him with a big smile.

"Mind if I join you?" Cal boarded the golf cart and told her to take them down to the lake.

Feet up and relaxed, they sat for a while looking out across the large lake that bordered both properties. It was like looking over the past and peering into their shared connections. They'd always been connected and now that he thought he was falling in love with Chloe, Cal longed to move forward in their relationship, forging new connections and making new memories. Hell, he thought he might be ready to talk marriage with her. Encroaching into his thoughts was Chloe's soft voice, asking what was on his mind.

He turned to her and lifted her hand. "I need to tell you something about the night we hooked up in Vegas."

Chloe tilted her head that way she had, the way that told him she was listening with her heart as well as her ears. "Okay, shoot."

"Babe, I was quite intoxicated. You were intoxicated. I can't say I'm sorry about any of it because I've grown to not only want you, but need you. You're all I think about these days. I would never knowingly hurt you. You know that, don't you?"

Chloe sat up straighter. "Cal, you're scaring me. What's this about?"

"It's nothing for you to worry about, but I wanted you to know there was a bet . . . a bet that had been made."

Her forehead furrowed. "What kind of bet?"

"A bet involving you."

Chloe pulled her hands from Cal's grip. "Okay, I figured that, but just how does it involve *you?*"

Cal looked out across the lake. "I inadvertently bet Cory, Dean, and Bradley that I could get you in the sack that night."

Chloe's eyes narrowed and her luscious lips tightened into a thin line. "The word *inadvertently* is a nice touch." She angled herself toward the water and he could no longer see her eyes. "Then I'd say you won that one quite a few times over. Tell me, how much is my body worth?"

Cal leaned forward and searched Chloe's face. Her eyes were filled with tears. He reached for her, but she pulled away. "Chloe, I didn't collect." Thank God he hadn't.

"How much Cal?" Her voice was getting louder.

"Five hundred dollars, but as I said, of course I didn't collect. I put a stop to it immediately."

"Is that supposed to make it all better?"

"No." What else could he say?

Chloe shook her head. "I *knew* it was too good to be true. I knew it. My sister said I was crazy for dating you after all the shit you did to me when we were young, but I told her it was different now. I said we really cared for each other, but obviously I was wrong."

Chloe was on her feet and walking back toward her parents' home. Cal leaped from the cart and ran after her. He wrapped one arm around her waist, and she immediately fought him with her fists. "Put me down, you bastard!"

"Not a chance. I need you to hear what I have to say." He threw her over his shoulder caveman style and walked her back to the cart, setting her gingerly on the back seat. "I can understand why you are hurt, and I was wrong to do what I did, but you were right to tell your sister that things are different now. They are different. I'm different. I think I may have actually fallen in love with you. I think I want to build a life with you. You have to admit that you feel our connection too."

He removed his hands from her shoulders and waited for her response. When she didn't speak, he started to pace on the patch of grass directly in front of her. "Say something."

Cal ducked just in time to avoid the nine iron that came at his head. It caught the fiberglass roof of the golf cart instead. Chloe didn't stop there. She swung several more times at the cart. Or maybe at him. She was erratic, so it was difficult to know her intent.

She yelled, "Caleb Dean St. Martin, I'll never let you touch me again! You *think* you want to build a life with me, you *think* you might love me! You don't have sex with someone the way we do unless you *know*, know for sure." She took another swing at his head. "I *knew* I fucking loved you, I *knew* I wanted to spend the rest of my life with you, and now I *know* I never want to see you again!"

"Chloe, don't do this!"

Her fists clenched and her eyes grew to narrow slits, as if she were looking out through a helmet. As if they were at war. "I didn't fucking do it, you did. Tell me, Cal, why are you telling me about the bet now?"

"I wanted to tell you before you heard it from the others."

"Right, but if you put a stop to it so immediately, why is it that you need to tell me before I hear it from someone else? Why does everybody know that you won the bet? Why would you even need to explain the reason you aren't collecting unless you boasted about it at some point?"

Cal winced at her questions. God, he hated to think what she would do when he told her he actually did boast about it, drunk-texting the guys that they owed him five hundred dollars.

Chloe sneered. "Not so talkative now, are you?" Chloe threw his father's prized Honma nine iron, now a mangled mess, into the lake and started to walk home.

35

"Please don't walk away from me." She didn't stop. "Chloe." He took one step after her. "Don't go."

She stopped and turned, her face red and angry. "Tell me how the guys knew you succeeded in your conquest."

He dropped his head, knowing that at his admission, Chloe would be gone from his life forever, casting him into darkness. "I texted them sometime during the night."

Gasping on a harsh breath and pulling herself up to her full height, she looked him square in the eye. "I hate you, Caleb Dean St. Martin, and I'll hate you till the day I die."

At those words, at her admission, Chloe turned and ran. The beauty of the landscape with its green and lush grasses, still lake, and ducks flying overhead was a stark juxtaposition to the events playing out in front of them. With Chloe gone, emptiness wrapped around Cal like a cloak. He dropped to his knees and scrubbed his hands over his face then tugged his hair as hard as he could. Through his own stupidity, he'd lost the only woman he had ever loved.

CHAPTER 5

Chloe spent the rest of the weekend at her condo in her pajamas. She ordered a large brick oven pizza and in two days, managed to eat it all. She caught up on all her reality shows, what her mother referred to as trash TV. She cried until she thought she'd get dehydrated, and her head was so stuffy it hurt like hell.

She was mad. Not just heartbroken, but angry.

She knew the moment she'd seen forever in Cal's eyes. It was when he'd said, *"Where you stand is next to me."* In that moment she had sensed a change in him. A meaningful change. Unfortunately she'd been mistaken, and he hadn't changed at all. She'd seen only a lie. She was still a source of amusement and entertainment. He didn't care one bit about her.

When the doorbell rang Sunday evening, she was tempted to ignore it, but she needed a break from herself and her thoughts. She looked through the peephole and into familiar ice-blue eyes. Shit. What was he doing here? She pulled the clip out of her hair and ran to her room to slide on a pair of jeans and a clean T-shirt. She ran a brush through her hair.

Another knock sounded at the door.

"Chloe, I know you're in there; I can see your car. Plus I can hear the TV."

Chloe clicked the television off and grabbed all the tissues from the coffee table and those peppering the floor around the couch. "Just a minute," she yelled at the door. She took the pizza box to the kitchen trash and wrangled it down using her fists and feet to bend it into submission. She glanced around and was satisfied she'd gotten rid of the evidence of her pity party and crying jags. Except her eyes still felt puffy. She grabbed the frozen spoon she kept in the freezer for that very thing and laid the cool metal delicately under her eyes as she walked toward the door. When she was content with how her eyes felt, she twisted the lock and turned the knob.

"Damn, woman, what the hell? It's hot as fuck out here."

She offered him a sickeningly sweet smile. "My apologies, but I don't remember inviting you here. What do you want?"

"What I want is for you to be reasonable and—" She tried to close the door, but Cal had wedged his food in the doorway. "Dammit, Chloe, I just came for the tapes."

Chloe froze as she thought about their project. Of course he would still complete it; he'd known the LeBlancs too. That made sense to Chloe, and she was happy he was going to complete the video. "Okay, come in."

He went to her desk and sat down. He looked like he planned to stay a while. Was he playing her again? She had to admit that he'd fooled her well and she no longer trusted her instincts when it came to him.

"What are you doing?" she asked.

"I've got to transfer the video footage I've already cut from your laptop to mine. It's going to take a while."

"Take it; I've got another laptop. You can get it back to me later."

His scent of expensive cologne and starch assaulted her senses, conjuring unwelcome memories. She needed him to leave now, before she became too weak to fight him off.

Too weak to fight herself.

"Chloe, it's not a big deal. I'll just transfer them to my hard drive."

Chloe's hands clenched at her sides, and her shoulders hunched. "I said take my laptop and get out."

Cal's shoulders tensed. A tic jumped in his jaw and he opened his mouth, but he said nothing. He sighed instead and pulled a box from his pocket, placing it on the kitchen counter. "I'm truly sorry I ever hurt you." He hoisted the box of tapes onto his shoulder and picked up Chloe's laptop. He started to walk out.

"Are you? How can I believe that? You've been hurting me my entire life."

Torrents of tears ran down her face. Her breath was erratic, and she clapped her hand over her mouth. Cal moved in on her, but she lifted her shaky hand in front of him and said, "Don't touch me." She wiped her eyes and then stepped close.

"It would be easy to forgive you, but where would it end? You've been treating me like your sworn enemy all these years when I've never done anything but love you." As her tears grew heavy, she gasped for air. "Do you even remember the things you did to me?" Her voice was low and lacked inflection. She stared at a spot off in the distance. "There was that time I'd gotten into a fire ant bed down by the lake. I was thirteen. I quickly took off my clothes and jumped into the lake to wash off the ants. I'd been stung repeatedly and my legs were on fire. I was in the lake when you showed up with your brothers." Her eyes grew glossy. "You took my clothes." Her gaze narrowed as she looked to Cal. "It was cold in the lake. I begged you to give my clothes back. But instead of giving me my clothes, you humiliated me in front of your brothers." Whisper quiet and with her head lowered, she said, "I had to step out of the lake naked. Yet you still wouldn't give me my clothes."

Cal's eyes closed. He shook his head.

She held her head high. "Tell me what happened next."

He choked off a sob, his eyes still closed, as if he couldn't bear to look at her.

"If you even remember." She shrugged. "I've never forgotten."

"You begged and pleaded once more for your clothes." His voice was raspy. "I teased you. We called you a wet chicken, and we crouched down to walk and flap like chickens. You ran naked all the way home."

"So you do remember."

Cal opened his eyes.

She crossed her arms across her chest. "I didn't think you did. You never speak about the mean things you did to me."

"Chloe, we were children. I will spend the rest of my life making those moments up to you if you'll just let me."

"We weren't kids in Vegas." She picked up the gift from the counter. "What's this?"

Cal shook his head and his shoulders slumped. "It's me trying to atone, but I don't think there is anything I'll ever be able to do to make it up to you. I'm sorry." A guttural groan was the last thing she heard as he walked away.

Chloe picked up the beautifully wrapped package and took it to the table. She swallowed the lump in her throat as she pulled at the bow atop the package and tore through the silver paper. She set the square white box on the table and removed the lid. Inside was a silver charm bracelet. She pulled it up and inspected each charm. There was a charm made up of three letters, SLP—speech language pathologist. There was a pair of lips and also a golf cart, a nine iron, an ice cream cone, and a chicken. The last charm her eyes landed on was the hand sign for *I love you.*

Chloe pulled out a card.

Chloe,

What I did was wrong. I would give my right arm to change everything about that night. Hell, I would give my life because I don't need it without you. If you think you might ever forgive me, I would spend the rest of my life making it up to you. I know I love you. I know I have always loved you, even when we were kids. I guess that's why I relentlessly teased you. Again, I'm sorry. It was never my intention to hurt you.

Cal

Chloe was numb. She dropped her head on her arm on the table as she thought about her relationship with Cal. She dozed off with the bracelet clasped in her hand, imagining what could have been. She dreamed about them, about their life together. They bought a house and lived in Whiskey Cove. It was the story she always used to write about in her journal, but now it came to life in her dreams.

She woke, startled, and was immediately aware of her stiff neck and shoulders. She saw her keys on the table and the heart clock read 6:30. Shit! Exhausted, she'd fallen asleep at the table, the weight of the jewelry in her hand reminding her of the night's events. As she palmed the bracelet, she recognized that she was still in love with Cal, with all that love entailed. He wasn't the boy of her youth. He had changed. He'd been solicitous of her needs and the needs of Riley and Sarah. She'd become teary-eyed watching him read a storybook with the girls, using different voices for the characters. When Riley had reached out to hug him, Cal had kissed her cheek, had told her she was a very special little girl. He genuinely cared for the LeBlanc family and had comforted Chloe through the difficult ordeal of Steve's illness. God, it killed her to relive those memories. He'd changed and while he still made mistakes, so had she. She wanted to forgive him. She would forgive him. She only hoped she wasn't too late.

At work, Chloe was preoccupied throughout the day. She'd worn the bracelet and couldn't wait to thank him properly for it. Her day at work had gone well. Steve had used her communication board to tell the girls he loved them. Sarah seemed to really understand how to use the board. As Chloe was leaving his room, Steve's gaze went to the words *thank you* and to the picture of Chloe on the board. She had to leave the room before she broke down and cried like a baby, upsetting the LeBlanc family.

She needed to see Cal and when she got off, she drove straight to his apartment. As she pulled up alongside his truck, she realized she didn't even have a change of clothes. *And* she was in her ugly green hospital scrubs. There was no way she was going home now, so she exited her 4Runner and hurried up to his door. She pressed the doorbell and heard him moving around behind the door. As soon as he opened the door, she was in his arms, with him murmuring her name over and over into her ear. He held her close, her legs wrapped around his waist and her arms around his neck. He kissed her passionately and she cried.

Cal wrapped her cheeks in his palms. He whispered, "You came back to me."

Tears swam in Chloe's eyes. "I love you."

"God, am I dreaming? You know how much I love you, right?"

Chloe nodded.

"I'm sorry about the bet; I never meant to hurt you."

"I know."

"And all that stuff I did to you when we were kids? I think I only did it because I didn't know how to handle the feelings I had for you even then."

Chloe locked one hand in his hair and stared into his eyes, "I know. You were right, we were children. There was always a fire surrounding us, a passion I only feel when I'm with you. We will still make mistakes but reading in your note that you always loved me and that you'll spend the rest of our lives making me happy, well, what more can I hope for? You've given me everything." She tipped her forehead against his heart. "You are everything."

Cal went to his knees, wrapped his arms around her waist and squeezed her to him. "God, I thought I'd lost you." His eyes closed, and he rubbed his face across her stomach. "I will do everything in my power to keep you happy. I'll try to do it perfectly, but I'm only human and I know I'll fall short, but I need you to understand—I won't ever intentionally hurt you. I love you. Please, I need you to know that in your heart." He squeezed her hips. "In your body." He gazed up at her. "In your soul."

Chloe held his face in her hands and tenderly brushed a shaking finger over his lips and then his eyes. He leaned into her hands. When she encouraged him to lift his head again, she smiled. "I know that now. And I certainly don't expect perfection. Look at me. I almost destroyed the best thing in my life simply because I let my temper fly at a misunderstanding, because I wouldn't allow you to explain. If you can tolerate my actions, I can certainly do the same."

"Let's start fresh, the past behind us."

She smiled and nodded. "The past behind us."

***

Cal's apartment was loft style and overlooked downtown Baton Rouge. The wall the bed rested against was made of exposed brick. He wondered if it would be unseemly to get Chloe into that bed soon.

"Cal, do you think I can borrow something to wear."

His brow rose as she kicked off her track shoes and pulled the scrub top over her head and shimmed the bottoms down. She wore thong panties to the hospital? "Can't you walk around in your underwear?"

Chloe grinned. "I suppose I can, but I thought we might order Thai food. I could see if they offer a discount for answering the door in your underwear. That, or I could get arrested for indecent exposure."

He tossed a white oxford shirt at her head. She unclasped and removed her bra. Her eyes cut to him, and she gave him a saucy smile, knowing she had his full attention. She raised the shirt over her head and slid into it without undoing the buttons. As her hips danced provocatively, the shirt slid down her silky skin. When she was done, Cal stood directly in front of her with a camera on a tripod.

"Can I record you?"

Chloe shrugged. "What do you want me to do?"

"Just be yourself." He knew he'd never capture her essence, but he'd been wanting to film her, knew her image on the screen would be breathtaking.

"Okay."

She walked to her purse and pulled out her brush. Unclipping her hair, she let it cascade down her back and slowly, sensually, she brushed it out. Each curl pulled straight by the brush before bouncing back into place. Once she was done she smiled up at the camera. Then she set about taking in his apartment. He followed her with the camera.

"Geez, Cal, you've got an awful lot of equipment."

She went to his bookcase to peruse his music collection. She found his iPod on a dock and thumbed through hitting play on Radiohead's "High and Dry". She then checked out all the family photos. Once she made it to his bed, she lowered herself to the edge. Pushing with her arms, she slid back to the middle. One of her legs was bent at the knee and the other was pointed straight at Cal and his camera. She leaned back on her elbows, allowing the hair behind her to cascade down her back like the falls of a silver-white river. He loved her hair. Had told her so many, many times.

"Put the camera on the tripod and come over here," she said, her voice breathy.

Cal did as he was told. He crawled up Chloe's body as he unbuttoned the shirt she wore, parting it to expose her full breasts. He kneaded and sucked them gingerly before he dipped his head between them, suckling at the flesh there until he left his mark.

"Hey, stop that now."

"Chloe, you're mine. You must bear my mark."

Grinning, she pulled his cotton T-shirt over his head. "Tit for tat."

She sucked at his chiseled chest, then checked out the effect. Her mark didn't leave much contrast on his bronze skin.

"I like your jeans," she told him.

He wore a very worn pair of faded jeans that had holes across the knees and thighs. He knew the kinds of looks he got from women when he wore the jeans to run errands. Didn't know why they liked them, but that didn't mean he was unaware. But now he was more interested in what Chloe was wearing. He hooked his thumbs into her panties and slid them down her legs ever so slowly.

Leaving her shirt on but open to expose her breasts, he pulled her to the edge of the bed and positioned himself between her legs. He rose up and checked the angle of the camera. "I want to capture the look on your face when you come." A blush crept across her body and chest, and her eyes smoked out. She was fucking gorgeous already, but like this she was a goddess. He knelt between her legs. "Put your legs over my shoulder and move that impressive ass to the edge of the bed."

Chloe did as he said. As soon as she was spread for his view, he groaned and used his fingers to spread her wide. First he simply drank her in with his eyes. Then he inhaled, taking in her essence. Then his tongue licked up her seam. He wedged his shoulders between her legs, spreading her wide. Using his fingers to open her lips, he fucked her with his tongue and rasped his cheek across the exposed flesh of her sex. He went at her like he was consuming his last meal, loving her taste. Loving her breathy moans.

Chloe's fingers dug into his hair and she pulled at it just enough to drive him wild. She planted her feet on his shoulders and thrust herself up to his mouth. When his teeth grazed her clit, she moaned around his name. He continued to eat at her as if he were devouring the sweetest and juiciest ripe peach until she cried his name and writhed beneath him. When she came, he lapped up all of her tangy juice.

Cal pulled his face away from her and wiped his mouth and cheeks across her thigh. At that, Chloe groaned and reached for him. He stood and undid his pants, sliding them down his thighs.

Her voice was a whispered rasp when she said, "What are you doing?"

"I'm taking off my pants because I'm going to fuck you now."

Her eyes went wide. "No boxers?"

He smiled. "Commando."

His erection was hard and reached to his navel. After he'd loved Chloe's pussy, it was painfully aroused. She watched him, and her tongue darted out from between her teeth to lick her lips.

"Do you like what you see, Miss Mills?"

Lashes lowered, she simply responded, "Mmm."

Cal grabbed his cock and stroked himself from root to tip until Chloe moaned impatiently. He waited until she grew restless, then he crawled up her body, raised her knees, and tilted her ass so he could see all of her. He rubbed his cock through her moist center and used his hands to guide himself inside, pushing to the hilt. Chloe cradled his hips with her thighs. When he moved, she moved. When he slowed, she slowed. They were in sync. She opened her eyes, noticed the mirror on the ceiling. He felt her core flood with moisture.

Cal watched her eyes widen and then become hooded. "Tell me what you see, Chloe."

"The light rolls off your muscles when you flex your hips."

He plowed deeply into her, and she greedily absorbed everything he had to give. They came together when her tight walls squeezed his orgasm from him. They stayed connected as they came down from the height of passion, the camera still rolling. Cal was lost in the depths of her passion filled eyes.

"Chloe, I love you."

"I love you too." Her voice was hoarse when she echoed him.

Cal grasped her wrist and pushed the shirtsleeve up, kissing her wrist. "I'm glad you're wearing the bracelet."

Chloe smiled.

After eating and more sex to celebrate their newly declared love, they lay in bed, just talking. And stroking one another. And smiling. At least he was.

They fell asleep without fuss, with Cal only waking when a clunk sounded in the darkness.

Chloe pulled out of his arms.

"Hey, where are you going?"

"My phone fell from the stand. It's buzzing on the floor."

Cal reluctantly let her go. She reached for the phone and he turned on a light. She silently scrolled through the messages. Cal sensed what was coming.

He sat up in the bed behind her. "What is it?"

"Steve passed away. About thirty minutes ago."

She curled into Cal's chest. Her cries started as quiet whimpers, eventually becoming agonized gasps. Cal held her while she grieved. Two hours later she'd quieted and lay dozing in his arms. He laid her head on a pillow and got up to make a pot of coffee. He pulled pastries out of the freezer and heated them in the oven. Then he drew a bath and went to Chloe, pulling the shirt from her body. He carried her to the bath and slowly lowered her into the warm water. He slid in behind her.

He gently washed her hair and her face and shoulders, kneading as he went. Then he washed the rest of her. When he was satisfied, he stood, leaning Chloe against the side of the tub. He retrieved a fluffy white towel from the cabinet and helped her out. He dried her with tenderness, leaving kisses all over her body. He even dressed her. He was beginning to worry that she had gone into shock since she was completely unresponsive, but when he placed a coffee cup in front of her, she sipped from it. Cal knew they needed to get to the hospital. He planned to not leave her side for a second in case she needed something. Anything. He would be there for Chloe. Forever.

CHAPTER 6

The days after Steve's death had all rolled into one until Chloe had no idea how long it had been. Cal had been wonderfully attentive to her needs. Steve's death had breathed new life into his project and she'd watched him diligently work on the video. Mike, his professor, mentor, and lead on his thesis committee, had come to the apartment to view his work and listen to Cal explain the project. It was clear Mike was blown away by the work he'd already done. Chloe didn't quite understand how it was to all come together since it was still in the editing phase and resembled nothing of a documentary. Mike told him he had a real shot at winning the Independent Film Fest's documentary feature film category. And then he went on to say that if Cal were to win, it would have Hollywood calling.

As Mike was leaving, he said, "Be sure to upload your video by the fifteenth. I'm serious—you've got a real shot with this, Cal. Judges love it when you pull at the heart strings."

Cal had been understandably excited. But Chloe was confused and upset, not sure what Mike had meant.

Cal, behind Chloe, wrapped his arms around her. He kissed her cheek and pressed close.

"Hey, are you feeling better?" he asked.

"Are you going to enter that film festival?"

"Yeah, I think so. Did you hear what he said? With this story I've got a real shot at winning."

"Cal?"

"Yeah, baby."

"I don't want you to enter Steve's battle in some contest, not for personal gain."

He released Chloe and moved around her, even as she turned, to look into her face. His eyes were wide. His cheeks flushed.

45

"How can you even think that's what I'm doing?" He stepped back and crossed his arms. "Chloe, you should think about what you say before you say it."

When she didn't say anything, at least not fast enough to suit him, he turned and started putting on his shoes.

"Where are you going?" Had she mistaken his intentions? It hadn't sounded as though she had. Mike wanted him to feature the documentary about Steve in a contest. Her ears worked pretty well.

Cal wouldn't answer her, not even when she asked again. He stood, lips tight and hands clenched at his sides. Then he tilted his head forward and rubbed at his neck. It made a horrible popping sound. He slid his keys from the bowl he kept on a console table by the door and walked out.

He simply walked out.

Chloe cried for a while, but then she got angry. She wondered if Cal had used her yet again, used her to get close to Steve. Now that she thought about it, that was when their relationship had started getting serious—right after he came to the hospital that first time. He'd told her about his thesis project after he'd offered to help with the video editing. Chloe felt sick to her stomach. She ran into the bathroom and spilled the contents of her stomach into the toilet. She collected her things and left his apartment.

Later that evening, there was a knock at Chloe's door. She knew it would be Cal, but she didn't want to see him. She didn't want to be reminded of the traitorous things he'd done. Through the door she said, "Go away, Cal."

"Chloe, don't be childish. Open the door. We need to talk."

"Childish!" Chloe yelled, yanking at the door handle.

Cal strode inside. "Have you come to your senses?"

"Not even close."

"So you agree that you're being unreasonable."

Chloe shook her head, slamming her hands to her hips. "What? No. You mixed up my words."

"The video isn't about the contest, it's about telling Steve's story. If you don't think I'm professional enough to do that, then you don't know me. And maybe we shouldn't be together."

Chloe threw her hands in the air. "If it isn't *about* the contest, then why do you need to enter the contest?"

His voice was louder, his temper evident, when he said, "Are you listening to me? I said it's about telling Steve's story. The contest is a way to reach millions of people."

"It's not the only way." Chloe was getting louder too. "The contest is about you exploiting Steve just like you exploited me for your own personal benefit."

Cal's brows drew together and his lips tightened. "Son of a bitch," he whispered, throwing his arms wide. "I can't win here. I've bent over backwards trying to undo the wrong I've done to you." He glared at her with a fixed gaze. "Yet you still haven't forgiven me. What do I have to do? And now . . . Now you accuse me of exploiting a dead friend for gain." He threw his hands over his head. "I can't remember a time when someone insulted me—no, hurt me—more than you just have."

He pressed his palm to her cheek. "I deserved your anger, but it's clear the damage has been done and is irreparable. For the record, I'm not the kind of man who would take advantage of people he loves for his own gain. I would rather have nothing than to get ahead in that way. I saw enough of Dad's competitors take that route—it sickened me as a kid and it sickens me now. And it cuts me deep that you, of all people, don't believe that." He headed to the door. "That you don't know that about me. That you . . . that you believe me capable of such betrayal and deceit." He dropped his head with his hand on the door, and took in a long breath. Then he looked over his shoulder with glassy eyes. "Goodbye, Chloe. I hope your future is better for you than the past has been. I hope the next man who loves you does it right, right from the beginning. I wish it would have been me."

He opened the door and walked out.

Chloe stood in the center of her living room in a state of shock. The man she loved with everything she had just walked out on her. For the last time. She'd read the resolve in his face. He wasn't coming back.

She cried herself to sleep on the floor of her living room.

The next few weeks at work were bleak for Chloe. Memories of Steve were everywhere. To make matters worse, memories of Cal plagued her body. Visions of him from the mirror above his bed as he plowed into her would come to her at the most inopportune times, like when she was out to lunch with her mother. She would daydream about the erotic movements made by the flex of his hips and the way the light rolled off his taut muscles whenever he thrust into her.

And when she huddled in her bed, unable to sleep, visions of him smiling and laughing and working hard on his thesis haunted her.

But it was his eyes, his eyes filled not only with tears but with pain, that really haunted her. She couldn't get that final image of him, that picture of him standing at her door and suffering from her betrayal, out of her mind.

Chloe was finishing up her charts at the nurses station when Nancy, the head nurse, stepped up next to her and laid her laptop on the counter. "Caleb St. Martin brought this by. He asked me to give it to you."

It was the last blow. Chloe gathered up her laptop and left. She was in for a night of gut-wrenching grief. She stopped by a local wine store and selected four bottles to keep on hand. She planned to down the first one tonight. With a king-sized bar of chocolate.

Chloe was utterly devastated that Cal had returned her laptop via Nancy.

She'd seen the smirk on the woman's face. Everyone knew they'd broken up.

She'd thought in these last weeks that she might have been wrong about Cal, so she just couldn't understand why he wouldn't pull the damned film. She wondered if the situation were reversed if she would have let it come between them. She hoped she wouldn't have.

Once she got home, she opened her returned laptop and loaded Netflix. She wanted to watch a good comedy. That was when the file on the top right of the screen caught her eye.

Click Me.

Chloe clicked the icon. Aqualung's "Thin Air" played as pictures of her flashed on the screen; he'd found photos from her childhood, pictures of them together: a fall hayride, a Christmas parade, and her birthday party. She remembered that picture. He'd given her a Polly Pocket and she was ecstatic. There were pictures of her on his eighteenth birthday wearing her black strapless dress. He'd taken them on the front porch of his home. One showed her on the swing with her legs drawn up underneath her—there were eight candid shots of her from that night. She hadn't known he'd taken them. He'd added captions. The one on the swing read: "The moment I knew Chloe Mills would be burned into my memory forever." There was one of her walking in the high grass as she carried her pumps wedged between her index and middle fingers: "Genuine beauty comes in only one form—Chloe." There was a picture he'd scanned in, one he'd taken with the novelty camera she'd given him that night. It was a close-up of their heads together. He'd held the camera in front of their faces and taken the shot: "The moment Cal knew he loved Chloe."

He'd been right about that camera, it was shit.

Chloe cried, howling like a baby. The pictures changed to more recent ones. He'd included pictures of her with Steve and the girls and of her teaching them how to communicate with Steve.

The song's crescendo accompanied the footage of him making love to her on his bed. This was video, not stills, but he'd made it black and white. Her hair, the white oxford shirt of his that she'd worn, and her light skin were in stark contrast to the dark colors of his bedroom and his bronzed body and dark hair. The video was tastefully edited and showed no objectionable nudity, just unbridled passion and lust. She saw herself through his eyes and she was beautiful.

She writhed beneath him, and her eyes were darker than she'd ever seen them. She wouldn't have recognized herself. She was sexy and passionate, and for the first time, she realized why he could have been attracted to her. She was desirable. She saw it in herself but more than that, she saw it in him, in his eyes. They held admiration and reverence. They held love.

There were more pictures, of them attending the funeral and of her working with Steve. There was even a picture of her asleep. In fact there were several pictures of her in various sleepy poses. The video ended with her reading the Berenstain Bears to Sarah and Riley above the melodious hum of Matt Hales.

Chloe plugged in her headphones and listened to the Aqualung song over and over as she fell asleep. The words begin to seep through her skin and she felt them deep in her bones. She held no doubt that Cal had always been in love with her. His videos were not exploitive. They told a story just as clearly as if he'd written out the words.

In the morning, she showered and dressed and then drove over to his apartment. She pressed the doorbell and his cleaning lady answered. She remembered Cal had called her Mrs. Hall.

"Well, Chloe Mills, come on in."

"Good morning, Mrs. Hall. Do you know where Cal is?"

"He's out of town. Utah. For a film festival. Most of the family went with him."

"When did he leave?"

"I'm not sure about that, but I'm pretty sure he loves you. He couldn't stop talking about you. Did you know that?"

Chloe smiled at the middle-aged woman. "Yes, I believe I did know that. Thank you."

Chloe did a little sleuthing—she found out from Alyssa that the festival was in Park City—and then she called the airline and bought a ticket to Utah. She hoped she wouldn't be too late to see Cal's début. She hoped that all the way there, in between bouts of figuring out what she'd say to him.

Once the plane landed, she called Cory. He helped her arrange a taxi to Park City and a hotel room in Salt Lake. Their plan was simple: Cory would save her a seat at the premiere and she would surprise Cal. In her hotel she primped and waxed, wishing she could have saved time by doing it on the plane. She had her hair professionally done at the hotel's salon. And then she carefully pulled on a peach-colored lace cocktail dress, pairing it with strappy sandals. She hurried to the waiting cab and arrived at the theater with thirty minutes to spare. She texted Cory, and in only a few minutes, he joined her in the lobby.

He gave her a warm hug. A strong brotherly hug.

"You look beautiful."

She smiled at him. He looked a lot like Cal tonight. But admittedly, the whole group of them were knockouts.

"Thanks, Cory."

"You know Cal's been a mess without you."

"Yeah, well, I've been a mess too."

With a raised brow, Cory asked, "So how do you want to play this?"

"Is he in there now?"

49

"Na, he's somewhere backstage tending to some last minute stuff."

"Well, I guess we could take our seats?"

Cory nodded. "As good a plan as any."

They walked down to the front of the small intimate theater. Cal's entire family had turned out and literally front and center, Clifton St. Martin stood beaming with pride. It had been a while since Chloe had seen the entire St. Martin clan. Cash had been winning big playing poker in Vegas—she'd actually seen him on television. And that's why Cal had been in Vegas that fateful night—to watch his brother play. Camp, Cash's twin, was busy working with his father at the St. Martin Contracting Company. Clay, the oldest brother, was a firefighter in Baton Rouge. She hadn't seen him in years. He'd always been muscular, but he seemed to fill out his suit even more now. Each brother hugged her and kissed her cheek. All of them seemed proud to be sitting in the theater to support Cal. His mother was seated at the far end of the row, next to the only other girl in the family, their sister, Clara. She was still in high school. Chloe waved because she couldn't get to them before the lights went down, and then the master of ceremonies came out on the stage.

Chloe took a seat next to Mr. St. Martin. He whispered in her ear, "Did you hear about my boy? I have a gut feeling about this. Without a doubt he is going to win this thing. He's too good not to."

His unwavering pride and confidence in Cal made Chloe's eyes fill with tears. "I couldn't agree more," she said.

He patted her leg with one of his large hands and turned to the stage.

The lights were turned down so quickly that it was difficult to see. But Chloe felt the energy from the body that dropped into the seat next to hers. She turned and whispered, "Cal."

He reached for her and roughly pulled her into his arms, lifting most of her body over the armrest. "God, Chloe," he whispered into her ear with a low, raspy voice. His hand snaked up to palm her head, loosening her professionally coiffed hair, but she didn't care. Cal's lips landed on hers with a ferocity that rendered her speechless. His tongue parted her lips, and he tasted her deeply. Chloe was glad the lights were turned down but even if they weren't, she wouldn't have stopped him. When their mouths relinquished one another, he continued to hold her close. "I need you. I knew you would be here." He squeezed her. "Thank God you're here."

"I'm here. I love you."

His breath escaped on a gasp, and he didn't hold back the lone tear that slid down his cheek. Chloe saw it glint on his face and wiped it away.

"I'm sorry for the things I said. I didn't know what I was saying. I believe in you, Cal. I trust you unconditionally."

"I know you do. I didn't explain. I should have explained."

"The "Thin Air" video you made . . . I can't—I don't—There are no words to tell you how much that video means to me."

They were forehead to forehead now.

"Chloe, you're here. That's all that matters. I love you. Always have. Always will."

***

The video started with a description of ALS. Medical specialists explained the disease's progression. After a brief history, including manifestation of the disease in its namesake, Lou Gehrig, current research in the field was explained. Cal had interviewed countless specialists, neurologists, and pathologists and clipped together segments about disease management and about the research still being done and the necessity of funding support to keep that research going.

Forty minutes into the documentary, clips of Steve were introduced. Still pictures of his early life played across the screen while facts about the disease ticked across underneath them—average survival time once diagnosed, average age at first diagnosis, percentage of people diagnosed each year. The facts were staggering. The effect of pairing a man's life and his experience with the disease *with* those facts was even more dramatic. Toward the end of the film, video clips of Steve in the hospital, with his family, played out.

Several moments of Chloe teaching Steve and his family to use the communication devices were included. Her voice filled the theater. The ticker on the bottom of the screen read: *Chloe Mills, Speech Language Pathologist, giving Steve a voice where otherwise he would have had none.* The documentary ended with video of Steve using the boards Chloe had made to tell his family he loved them. Using eye gaze, he communicated to each of his girls to give him a kiss and a hug. The video zoomed out on the image of Sarah and Riley, smiling, tenderly kissing Steve's cheeks.

When the lights came up, those in the audience, including every one of Cal's family members, were drying their eyes.

Cal and Chloe emerged from the theater, and people crowded around them. Several prominent actors asked where they could make donations. Cal looked to Chloe. She told them to make checks payable to the ALS Foundation. Several also made donations directly to the LeBlanc family. After the last patron left, millions of dollars had been raised for ALS research and to benefit Steve's family. Chloe was so overcome with emotion and exhaustion that she slumped against Cal and he had to help her out of the theater.

They rode in a limousine back to his hotel suite. Chloe lay in his lap, and he stroked her hair while she rested her head under his chin. His video wasn't exploitive at all. Chloe thought about what he'd said—she should have trusted him as a professional. She should have trusted him, period. She remembered what she had told him the night he left and winced at how truly horrid her words were. She'd maligned his work and his honor. She'd been bitchy and shortsighted and needlessly cruel. She'd let her insecurity hurt him. *She'd* hurt him.

"Cal, I don't know how you can forgive me for what I said that night. I think the videos you make are beautiful and haunting. They tell a real story, a touching story. They break down walls and lay bare the raw emotion in every scene." Tears escaped her eyes. Cal kissed them away.

"Chloe, that was a difficult time—you were grieving. You didn't understand, and I didn't try to help you understand. I just got angry. Just like I did when my father didn't understand. You've taught me so much about myself, about who I am and what I value. You make me whole. Look at how different my life is now that I've let you in—I'm reunited with my father and he came to see my film. Steve's story is heartbreaking but because of you, some good will come from his struggle. And because of you, I get to be instrumental in that. I can never make you understand what that means to me."

"Cal?"

"Yeah, Chloe?"

"I need you."

They were headed to Salt Lake City. Chloe knew they had about thirty minutes. Without speaking, Cal engaged the limo's privacy barrier. He slid Chloe's dress up her thighs to rest at her waist. He let out a groan when he looked at her.

"God, Chloe, you're not wearing panties."

She smiled. "Commando."

He blinked at her. She shrugged.

"Can't wear underwear with this dress."

"We need to buy you lots of these dresses." His voice was filled with lust.

She helped him unzip his trousers, and her small hands wrapped around his warm, full cock. She straddled his thighs and used her hands to guide him to her core. She rubbed his cock through her folds and inserted just the tip into her heat. He felt wonderful inside her, but she needed more. She pushed her palms into the limo's ceiling for leverage and pushed, lowering herself on his erection. She always had trouble taking all of him, but damn, she enjoyed the fullness when she did.

When he was fully planted inside her, Cal exhaled long and low.

"You're mine, Chloe. You belong with me. You—body, dreams, and heart—fit me like a glove." He licked and sucked at her neck, then he grabbed her ass and took them down to the floor. With him on his knees, he lifted her ass and placed her legs around his waist. They fucked so hard the limo rocked. Within minutes, Chloe gasped and called his name. Their eyes were locked on each other as her body convulsed, drawing his orgasm pumping out of him.

EPILOGUE

Sixteen videos vied for the top prize in the category of U.S. Documentary. He thought he'd heard his name but the scene played out as if in slow motion. Chloe elbowed him.

"Cal, it's you. They called for you."

He jogged toward the podium. He hadn't prepared a speech, didn't feel anyone should ever prepare a speech for an awards ceremony. He wanted to speak from the heart and since Chloe filled his heart to overflowing, he had an idea of what his speech would entail.

As he reached the podium with the glass award in his hands, he held it up and said, "This is for you, Steve."

His throat burned and knotted with emotion. He cleared it and said, "Behind every great man is always an even greater woman. This, of course, is the case with this film. This project only exists because of Chloe. Because of her I now understand the value of life, the value of family in ways I'd never envisioned. Chloe, please come up here and stand next to me."

Her smile looked a little shaky, but he guessed it was the emotion. She joined him and when he put his hands on hers, time stood still. It was just the two of them.

"Chloe Mills, I love you as I've never loved anyone or anything." He dropped to one knee. "Marry me, Chloe." He pulled a ring box from his pocket, cracked the lid, and offered it to her. Chloe's hands pitched over her face as the tears started to flow. " I'd give you my last breath if it would make you happy." She grasped the box and threw herself into his arms. They kissed on a stage, with his family and hundreds of strangers watching, a public commitment a lifetime in the making. The audience cheered, and Chloe's gaze scanned the audience. She turned her tear-stained face to Cal and offered an embarrassed smile. Cal angled them toward the audience and leaned into the microphone.

"I don't know for sure, but I'm thinking that's a yes?" His lifted his brow as he waited for her reaction. She moved toward the microphone and responded with a breathy, "Yes, I want to stand next to you forever."

The audience erupted in whistles and cheers. Cal and Chloe exited the stage hand in hand, bodies touching and hearts linked. Cal understood the significance of her words and he contentedly smiled as his body hummed with warmth, as it always had when Chloe was near.

***

EXCERPT *SHAMELESS*

Corrigan St. Martin was balls deep in his client's owner as he had her bent over the examination table and plowed into her from behind. Cory was about to come and judging by the moans coming from Mrs. Simms, she had to be just about there too. She was married, and he shouldn't have responded to her eye-fucking him, but damn, when she'd bent over to place her cat on the table, he'd lost it. She wore a silk lace undershirt, and her breasts nearly spilled out onto the examination table with the cat. She was natural, and Cory loved that. His dick had gone hard instantly. He wondered what kind of idiot she was married to. The guy obviously wasn't aware of what he had.

Cory reached around and filled his hands with her soft shapely tits and pounded away, emptying his seed into the condom he wore. He hated the damn things but at the rate he was having sex, he couldn't afford to not wear them.

Since he'd been back in Whisky Cove, he'd been set up with an endless supply of women. They had brought in their pets for "checkups." Hell, even at church the Southern mamas threw their daughters at him. It was no secret that the St. Martin men were a catch, if one could be snagged. The only one hitched now was Cal, the youngest at twenty-six. Cory had a year on him.

There was no way Cory would let himself be roped by a nagging wife; he had too much of a good thing going. Plus he didn't need that aggravation. He recalled Camp's issues with his first wife and those with his current girlfriend, soon to be fiancée. He thought Camp was crazy. Determined to be married and settled, he'd committed to a woman the church elders had deemed "quite the catch" just because she came from an old-money family and had a strong standing in the community. But that couldn't be enough, at least not for Cory. Standing and money, no matter how high or how deep, meant nothing if the woman was a ballbuster. Cory had no interest in marriage. Trying to keep a woman happy proved damn near impossible. Even his father hadn't been able to do it. Cory grunted; now he was thinking of his mom. Not the time for that. He thrust deep, trying to clear his mind. Just thinking of his mother roiled his stomach.

He recalled the day she'd left and the gut-wrenching pain she'd caused as he'd begged her not to leave. He'd been twelve and she'd been immune to his cries. Too bad he hadn't been immune to her defection.

And there he was, thinking of her again. He tweaked Mrs. Simms nipples, trying to keep his mind on business. When she moaned, he knew he'd done something right.

He'd been called the most handsome of the St. Martin men, but he didn't buy it. They all had the trademark St. Martin ice blue eyes fringed in dark lashes, something the ladies loved. They also seemed to love his hair. He was tempted to chop it off but when woman after woman locked fingers in it when he rode them, he didn't want to mess with a sure thing. The looks, coupled with his height and muscle, meant he never had to work too hard to have a woman visit his bed.

He'd lost count of the number of different women he'd given it to since his return from college last year. He was having sex daily, some days multiple times, and with a different woman every time. Nice-looking women too. He asked no questions, but he knew some of them were married, like Mrs. Simms, who was currently in the throes of orgasm.

Once Cory finished, he withdrew from Mrs. Simms, removed the condom, and threw it in the waste bin. He washed his hands while she adjusted her clothing. Opening the examination room door, Cory cleared his throat. "Mrs. Simms, bring the little guy back in four weeks for the next round of vaccinations."

Cory walked from the room and was straightening his tie when he met the tortured green eyes of a young woman holding an Airedale terrier in her arms. She sniffled as large fat tears splashed from her eyes and onto the dog.

Cory motioned her to the back examination room. Since it was time to close, his secretary, and one of his first conquests since coming home, was closing up for the day.

"Cory, she hasn't checked in."

Why was she still here? He'd told her to leave when he'd discovered the school bus had dropped off her two heathen children. She never disciplined them and she allowed them to run amuck in his clinic, treating the maze of exam rooms as a playground. Her mother must have come for them because if they were here, he'd certainly hear them.

"That's okay, Amanda, I'll take care of it. Lock up when you leave."

Truth be told, Amanda's fake tan, fake tits, and fake platinum hair gave

Cory the chills now, and her shrill voice made his skin crawl.

She sighed louder than necessary. "Okay, Cory, you have a good one."

To claim Cory as hers, Amanda had tried all the tricks women try when attempting to get their hooks into a man. One morning Cory was answering email at his desk and the crazy woman walked into his office in a raincoat and nothing else. He'd told her the ploy was pathetically cliché. She'd offered to suck him off under his desk and unfortunately, he'd let her. Since then she'd become clingy, and that was when Cory made his rule: no serial dating. Actually it was no serial fucking, sucking, dry humping, or any other form of passion that led to climax.

Since he'd been engaging in casual sex with so many other women, Amanda had cooled her jets.

Cory walked into the examination room where the young woman and dog were waiting. She was seated in the only chair in the room, rocking the Airedale.

Her luminous large green eyes looked up to him. "He needs to be euthanized. His usual vet was closed for the day. Please help me."

Cory knelt in front of the woman and petted the dog. "What's his name?"

"Randy."

"Hey, Randy," Cory said as he stroked the dog's head. Randy raised his eyelids and looked to Cory. Then he closed his eyes and winced. Cory saw the large tumor between his legs. Given its size, Cory guessed it must be interwoven into Randy's internal organs.

His owner was crying silently, tears streaking down her lightly freckled face.

"I can offer pain management, but I assume he's on medication already."

She nodded, her eyes fixed to the floor. "The meds were managing his pain until today."

"He's old."

She nodded again, her head lightly resting on the dog. "Seventeen."

"That's a full life for a dog. Damned good life. If you want to say goodbye, I can give you some time, and then I'll take him."

"No!" Her head rose as her brows slanted inward and her eyes grew wide. "I want to hold him when you do it." She kissed Randy. "I need to hold him."

Cory's head tilted as he studied her. "Uh, I don't think that's a good idea."

She squeezed her eyes shut and bowed her head. Her long chestnut hair, with copper highlights that sparkled under the florescent lights of the exam room, hid her face.

"You don't understand. Randy has been there for me. Always. He's the only remaining link between my parents and me. He was our family dog. We got him when I was seven." She stroked the dog's back. "I can't let him go out alone. I'll be here with him."

He'd seen this woman around his brother's brewery. She worked there on weekends, but kept to herself. She wasn't like the other women who worked there, definitely not like the one who'd actually groped him under the table; he'd had her in the bathroom. Had never even gotten her name.

The chestnut-haired beauty's distress weighed on him. And not only because her body heat reached out to him when he crouched in front of her. "I've seen you around. You work at The Good Doctor."

"Yes." Her head rested on Randy's as she continued to rock him.

"I didn't get your name."

"Brook Walker."

"Brook Walker." Cory's eyes turned wide as he recalled what he'd read about her in the Whisky Cove Herald. "The Brook Walker that rescues greyhounds from the race park?"

She nodded. "That's me."

Cory's mouth opened on a whispered "Wow." His gaze fixed on her. She'd rescued dozens of dogs and found them homes with people deemed suitable owners of a rescue greyhound. "You train them to be companion dogs, don't you?"

She nodded again, and this time a strangled cry broke from her lips.

It was killing him to see her like that, so he scooped Randy into his arms. "Come with me."

Brook was on her feet quickly. "What are you doing?" she demanded.

"I'm taking you and Randy out to my home, where there are stables and where we can all get comfortable, especially Randy."

Her brows furrowed as she shook her head. "What? Your home? I don't need you to do that; I just need him euthanized. Will you do it or not?"

Cory stopped at the door when it was clear she wasn't going to follow. "I can do that here on the stainless steel." He indicated the exam table with his head. "Or at a stable where we could lay him down on a bale of hay and let you take your time with him." Cory's body tensed. "Er, there's also the matter of the burial."

Her head cocked. "The burial?"

"Well, if you leave him here, he'll be cremated. It's the law."

She sucked in a quick breath.

"If you prefer a more peaceful resting place, there's a pecan grove at my childhood home. You could visit whenever you like."

She nodded as she thought through his words. "If it's not an imposition, I would greatly appreciate the pecan grove."

Cory tilted his head. "Don't mention it. It's the least I can do. After all, you put up with Logan at the brewery week after week." He walked her out to his SUV and motioned for her to open the rear door. He laid Randy gently on the seat, on an old blanket already lying there. He handed her the keys so that she could start the ignition. "Just let me grab a few things we'll need, and I'll be right back." She offered a tight smile this time with her nod.

As Cory was making his way back inside, her smile went with him. He thought of her full lips and the pretty white teeth that peeked through. He'd like to taste those lips. He grabbed the things he would need to put Randy in eternal sleep. He took a deep breath and released it slowly. He knew what Brook was feeling. He would do his best to make Randy's last moments as painless as possible for her.

Cory and Brook arrived at the gates of the St. Martin estate twenty minutes later. His father was in Lake Charles on business, so they would have the run of the place. Maybe he would grill some shrimp for them, if she felt like eating. She sat in the back on the ride over and murmured to Randy, words that Cory couldn't make out from the driver's seat. She truly was alone. He'd asked about her parents and discovered they'd both died. The story she'd shared about their deaths had reached out and grabbed him by the throat. He was determined to help her through the difficult night she had ahead of her.

Cory drove straight to the stables. He looked into the rearview mirror at Brook's red face, at the tears falling steadily. He parked in front of the stables and shifted to face her. He'd learned that no matter how painful, it was best to come clean regarding the events to come. Knowledge made things easier in the long run. "I suggest we get set up in the stables and, when you're ready, I'll administer the drugs." She was back to silently nodding.

Cory opened the rear door and removed Randy from her lap. Brook followed him into the stables. "Grab that blanket from the wall, will you?" Brook immediately complied. "Drape it across the bed of hay." Cory tried hard to not disturb the resting dog but when he laid him on the blanket, Randy opened his eyes and moaned. "There you are, old boy." Brook took the spot beside her dog.

Cory returned to his SUV for the black bag that held the drugs that would take Randy out of this world. The dog needed to be put down, but he knew it would be hard on Brook and he hated that she would forever connect him to her pain. He'd put down several animals since he'd opened his vet practice. Of course the owners grieved but they all did it differently. He wondered how Brook would do it. Usually, there were two grievers, two owners. Would Cory need to comfort her? The thought wasn't unpleasant to him, which he found odd. He shrugged.

Cory was glad the horses they usually kept were currently housed at his practice for breeding; they had the stables to themselves. He walked in and sat opposite Brook, leaving the dog between them. "I know you're aware that Randy is in a lot of pain. You're doing the right thing."

Brook's anguished green eyes met his. "Please, I'm ready."

Cory didn't say a word. He pulled the loaded syringes from his black bag and took Randy's paw into his hand and did what needed to be done.

Randy would be in a state of eternal sleep soon. His respiration was slowing.

Brook put her lips to his ear and said, "I love you, Randy. I'll miss you."

Cory wanted to give them privacy but when he rose to his feet, Brook grabbed his ankle.

He looked down and watched the tension ease from her tight shoulders on a deep exhalation of air.

"Will you stay here with me? Please. I don't have anyone else." Her lips trembled, and her sorrow filled the stable.

Cory wanted to comfort her, but he didn't know her, didn't know what she'd need. He lowered himself to the ground and sat quietly with her. Brook pulled Randy tight against her and leaned into Cory. His body immediately went rigid. He wasn't used to this kind of intimacy with women. Brook held Randy and lodged her head under Cory's chin. His body responded naturally. Without thinking, he snaked his arm around her waist. Her hair, smelling of wildflowers, tickled his nose and her bronze skin glistened in the glow of the overhead lights. Cory suddenly, urgently, wanted to taste that skin but he willed his desire down. The last thing she needed was Cory preying on her as though she were an animal in heat.

They sat quietly for about fifteen minutes. Rigor mortis would soon set in, and Cory didn't want Brook hugging Randy when it did. She hadn't moved since he'd placed his arm around her waist. To avoid startling her, he spoke softly into her ear. "I think we should talk about what you want to do next."

She turned her head to meet his eyes. "You mentioned a pecan grove?"

Cory smiled. "Yes, I think Randy would like it there; it's my favorite part of the property. Do you want to take him there now?"

Brook turned to look at the lifeless dog that lay across her lap. She whispered, "Okay."

Cory stood. "Let me get Randy, and you can help me gather some tools." He immediately loaded Randy into the Mule 4x4 and used a blanket to cover him.

He walked back in and directed Brook, just to give her something to focus on.

"Get the rake and the lanterns from that table." Cory motioned toward the table, and he turned to grab the shovel. He hoisted a bag of sodium hydroxide onto his shoulder. "And take a couple of those gray blankets from the shelf behind the table too." They loaded all the items into the

Mule and Cory drove to the garage. "I'm just gonna get some water." He leaped from the Mule.

Leaning against the refrigerator was a spear with white ribbon dangling from the tip. Cory snagged the stick to mark Randy's grave.

He drove them to the back part of the property and unloaded the tools. He should have changed clothes, but he hadn't wanted to leave Brook alone with her thoughts and her dog. It was hot, so he loosened his tie and removed it. His shirt followed. He started on the job of digging Randy's grave.

ABOUT THE AUTHOR

Gina Watson is author of the St. Martin Family Saga. She lives in Texas where she leads a double life: university instructor by day, romance writer by night. She loves to be contacted by readers to discuss all things romance.

Connect with Gina Watson online:
https://twitter.com/ginawatsongina
https://www.facebook.com/ginawatsonauthor
https://www.goodreads.com/user/show/6713553-gina
http://ginawatson.net/

Reviews: Please help spread the word. Review the book at Amazon, twitter, facebook, goodreads, or via email. Tag Gina so she can read your reviews and give her thanks.

Keep in touch: Join Gina Watson's email list at ginawatson@mac.com to receive alerts regarding sweepstakes, contests, giveaways, and upcoming book releases.

GINA WATSON'S BOOKS

ST. MARTIN FAMILY SAGA
SCORE
SHAMELESS
SHATTER
SUITED
SMOLDER

THE SAGA CONTINUES IN
THE EMERGENCY RESPONDERS TRILOGY:
SIZZLE
SECURE
SOOTHE

COMING 2014

Made in the USA
Charleston, SC
08 January 2014